Loving

Her

Holiday Hero

Beacon Bay Magic
Book 1

FIOLA FAELAN

Quicksilver Garou
primal passion

Loving Her Holiday Hero (Beacon Bay Magic – Book 1)
(Second Edition © 2023)
Published by:
Quicksilver Garou LLC
PO Box 5652
Beaverton, OR 97006

Cover & interior design by: Fiola Faelan
Cover photo licenses purchased & credit:
Beacon in circle: Depositphotos 156983526 ©katytutynina
Decorative separator: ©captainvector
Couple: iStock 1412858965 ©Liudmila Chernetska
Background: Depositphotos 172743004 ©2mmedia

Developmental Editing: Red Circle Ink
The author is responsible for any errors in the novel, no doubt having edited after the actual editors did their fine work.

Printed in the U.S. of A. on SFI, FSC or PEFC paper.
www.fioafaelan.com
ISBN (paperback): 978-0-9863273-5-3
ISBN (eBook): 978-0-9863273-6-0

Dedication

To my amazing son Cyrus and his equally amazing wife Molly—I can't tell you how much it means to me that you support and love me. I love you more!

I also have a wealth of support from actual blood-sisters to sisters-from-other-mothers, and even an informally adopted brother, not to mention amazing girlfriends. You ladies and gent know who you are.

I appreciate and love you all.

And to all those we love who have come before, and those who will come after—believe in the magic & power of love.

Content Alert

Domestic violence, mention of death of a child, explicit sex.

If you're new to the series...

THERE'S MAGIC IN LOVE... in those who've come before us, and those who will come after. There's magic in the sea, and in every civilization wondrous stories of magic abound.

In the Beacon Bay Magic series, you'll mingle with my characters in their small coastal town, built with my imagination—and their help. This fictional town is set on the Oregon Coast, in the beautiful Pacific Northwest in an area originally settled by the Siuslaw First Nations people, who inhabited it long before other folks arrived.

This fictional town is replete with magic, ghosts, and shapeshifters, causing folks with a raft of amazing abilities from around the world to gravitate to it—and there they stay. Druids from Ireland, magi from Persia, tribal goddesses, wizards, fairy-folk from Scotland, bruja from Spain, mediums, shapeshifters, warlocks, witches, and wizards. The list is endless and sometimes surprising.

Each person has abilities specific to their ancestry—magi from Persia can heal, detect danger to their loved ones, and craft protective wards around structures. Others from different ancestry can manipulate the ocean, wind, and storms. And yes, even shift into animals.

Beacon Bay is truly a psychic beacon to magical folk, for such an eclectic mix to trek there—each and every person pure of heart welcomed by the First Nations elders and healers—but only if they used their power for the good of the community. If these elders sensed evil intentions, they banished the person.

But... not all humans or paranormal-kind are banished before they wreak havoc on the community and inhabitants. Immerse yourself in their magical, mystical journeys as they fight to find-—and save—lives and love forever after.

Embrace the magic of love—Le Grá and Slàinte Mhaith

Blurb

This is a new edition, published with a new cover and edits to improve readablity and correct a few pesky errors.

***Features** a **brave** woman with a **battered heart,** a **sexy** protective hero, a **sweet** cherub looking for a mommy—and a **matchmaking grandma** from the **afterlife** replete with a **guaranteed HEA**!*

She hides behind her broken heart...

Natalie suffered a loss no mother should ever have to, and came out the other side vowing to keep her fractured heart locked away forever. Back in the magical town she grew up in, her plans to hide away in her gram's now empty home are foiled when a little girl suddenly appears on her porch, followed by the man she'd spent a week with years ago while standing vigil at her cousin's hospital bed. A man she'd held in her heart ever since. As her gaze locks on those gunmetal-gray eyes, recognition is instantaneous—and the attraction as electric as ever.

He'd fallen under her spell years ago…

Zach couldn't believe someone would snap at his little girl just because she'd suggested turning on Christmas lights. When he bounds up his new neighbor's porch steps to retrieve Belle, he comes face to face with the woman who'd burrowed into his mind and heart years ago—a woman he'd not been able to forget—and was shocked at the pain and sadness still radiating from the depths of her beautiful eyes.

Will she allow him to prove to her not all men have evil intentions, and open her heart to loving her holiday hero?

Chapter One

NATALIE SAT BOARD-stiff in the wicker rocking chair on the grand, wrap-around porch. The Christmas lights, twined around the railing and posts like candy-cane stripes, mocked her in their colorful cheerfulness, even unlit. She pictured Calum hanging them while their Grandma directed from this very rocking chair as she sipped peppermint hot chocolate.

When he came by later to visit, he could just unwind them and stick them back in the box. Natalie hadn't celebrated Christmas in three long years and wasn't about to start now.

Her hands ached, clenched around the skinny arms of the chair as dark memories threatened her hard-won peace, but she refused to succumb to the flashbacks she'd suffered her first year without Matty.

She'd conquered them, and wasn't by God going to fall apart just because of the stress of the move. Or the reminder that another Christmas was going to pass without Matty, and now without her beloved grandma.

Her shoulders bunched, her vision dimmed and her bones about rattled as she shook off being sucked into the darkness. Her gaze darted around to see if anyone caught her losing control in public, her eyes closing wearily as she sank back into the chair with a sigh.

When she dragged her eyes open again, she cringed to see one of the movers eyeing her as he walked past. No doubt he wished they could get the furniture moved and escape the prickly wacko spacing out on the porch.

She winced as she pushed to her feet, the fresh pink scar running the length of her right shin a stark reminder of her third surgery in as many years. She'd gone under the knife two months ago and it still pulled and ached.

At least there's muscle tone again. She stretched her foot carefully to a point, thankful she'd at least kept up with her physical therapy over the years. Not as if Calum would let her skimp on that.

"Why aren't your Christmas lights on? What's wrong with your leg?"

Her gaze snapped to the bottom step, and she felt her breath strangle in her throat to see a little cherub perched there, small fists on pudgy hips, accusing eyes fixed on the unlit string of lights.

She couldn't tear her gaze away from the almond-shaped, dark-chocolate eyes set in a cute-as-a-button face as the little girl clomped her way up the stairs on short chubby legs. Natalie's jaw ached from clenching her teeth, her fingers bleached of color as she gripped the porch rail. Her frantic heart tripped over itself like butterflies flitting against her breastbone, frantic to escape.

"I'm not turning them on. I'm taking them down."

The minute the words were out of her mouth, she regretted them. She'd never spoken harshly to a child before and didn't know why she'd done so now. The little girl didn't deserve her tone just for asking such an innocent question.

The porch shook as long, muscled legs took the three porch steps in one stride and a muscled arm snaked around the little girl's middle. Natalie's eyes jerked up to land on full lips, seamed shut in a hard line slashed across a fallen-angel face with warm toned, tawny skin framed by jet black, curly hair. Her eyes continued their trip up that harshly handsome face, to the sharp gray eyes, narrowed beneath dark brows, pinning her in place. Recognition slammed into her.

He looked just like she'd remembered, whenever she pulled him up in her memories—a throwback to some Aztec God. With his hair just brushing his collar, and his wide-as-a-bow shoulders straining a forest green polo shirt, he could model for the cover of 'Modern Warrior', if there was such a magazine.

Her gaze took in his sexy, washboard stomach clearly defined behind the tucked-in polo shirt, and narrow hips showcased in jeans that molded to muscular thighs.

At least ogling this handsome man beat back the last vestiges of her panic attack. It had been *years* since she'd looked twice at a man—since the last time she'd laid eyes on *him*—and only hours since she'd thought of *this* particular man.

The universe was completely screwed up if her libido awakened from its deathbed by her cousin's angry friend. The man she'd lusted after and thought of far too often since last they'd met.

A man with a child Matty's age when he was taken from her.

❅❅❅

ZACH COULDN'T believe his eyes. It had been barely a month since he'd moved to the small coastal town of Beacon Bay, settling into the old Victorian right next door. This house to the right of his, an old painted lady almost identical to his own, had stood empty and lonely the last few weeks, since the sweet old lady who'd lived there passed on.

He and his daughter used to enjoy hanging out with the older woman, his best friend Calum's grandma, while she played adopted grandma to his little girl. There were always cookies and milk available, along with entertaining conversation.

His buddy had mentioned just last week he'd have a new neighbor soon, however he'd failed to mention it was his cousin. The very woman Zach hadn't been able to forget since the day he'd met her while visiting Calum in the hospital, where he'd been recovering from a life-altering injury while overseas as Marine Special Forces. He'd hoped for a nice quiet family, with kids his daughter's age.

Instead, it was a woman who evidently wanted nothing to do with kids—not that he could blame her. He didn't have the full story, but knew she'd lost her little one years ago and was coping with that loss and subsequent surgeries from injuries sustained that fateful day.

Physically, she was looking better, except for her eyes—still as haunted as when he'd first met her. He could totally understand why, having no clue how a parent could survive the loss of a child with their heart or emotions intact.

Her mahogany hair flowed to her shoulders and framed a pixie face with cheekbones a model would kill for. Hazel didn't do justice to describe her eyes, gold bits sparkling amidst the green like glitter—her upper lip a sensuous cupid's bow, fuller than the bottom.

He ruthlessly pushed aside the burgeoning desire to know how it would feel to nibble on that lush fullness. Apparently, he was still as susceptible to her beauty and vulnerability as during the week in the hospital in Germany, watching over Calum.

If the clothes hanging on her slim frame were any sign, she'd lost weight. Some good old-fashioned Southern food would get meat back on her bones. Not that she wasn't drop-dead gorgeous just the way she was. He shook his head.

What was wrong with him, craving a lip-lock with someone who'd snapped at his little girl, and was apparently still dealing with issues he'd be better off staying as far away from as possible? He bit his tongue against offering sympathy and asking how she was as he snuggled his little sweetie against his shoulder.

"Hi, Natalie," he said softly. "It's good to see you again. Cal didn't mention you were our new neighbor. We're just next door. This is my daughter, Belle. She loves Christmas and just wants the neighborhood to be pretty. I'll make sure she doesn't bother you again." He turned to head back home, but the soft apology spilling from her full mouth had him turning back in surprise.

❄ ❄ ❄

"I'M S-SORRY, Zach—B-Belle. Truly. I didn't mean…" For the life of her, Natalie couldn't spit out another word. She'd bottled up too much for far too long, and to see the sympathy in his eyes on the heels of her grandmother's death, the move from Portland, along with the flash and fancy of the holiday drumming home the missing piece of her life, just did her in. She was on the edge of completely losing it. Of all places—in front of Zach, his child, and the movers—her emotions were going to pick *now* to fracture?

Her throat tightened as she choked back another sob and spun toward the front door, mortified to see a glint of sympathy in his sharp gaze turn into full on protector-mode. The heat of a broad palm on her shoulder was almost too much to bear.

"Hey, Nat? What can I do to help?" She felt a jolt of surprise to feel the rumble of his deep voice run right through that big warm hand to her shoulder, then on to the very heart of her. It was electric and sent tingles north and south through every nerve ending in her body. What the ever-loving heck was that about? She brutally cut off her reaction, knowing sympathy from this man would be her downfall.

She was a hairbreadth away from losing her composure and had to get into the house before she melted into a puddle of tears. She flung up her hand as the tears won, and with a jerky shake of her head, limped into the house and slammed the door in their faces.

Chapter Two

ZACH STOOD SPEECHLESS on the veranda. The heat of his attraction, along with sympathy at the shards of sadness and pain he'd glimpsed in her stunning hazel eyes, hit him square in the gut. Torn between giving her the privacy she so clearly desired, and intruding to see if he could help, Belle made the choice when her sticky fingers pulled his face around. "I have to pee, Daddy! Now!"

Zach dropped a kiss on his little girl's forehead and reluctantly turned away, loping down the steps and heading for his back door and inside to the closest bathroom before she left a wet spot on his hip.

He knew the basics of what had happened to Natalie, but wondered if something recent had occurred? She seemed shaky, was limping, and more emotionally fragile than at the hospital with Cal, although her loss was so recent back then, maybe she'd just been numb. He'd spend a week around her when they'd been taking turns keeping watch over her cousin. Although a cloud of sadness hovered over her during that time, he'd become reluctantly enamored of her.

She was brave and loyal, and her sense of humor would creep out when she tried to keep Cal's morale and mood up. It hadn't been the right time, though, since he'd been struggling as a single father, and knew there was no way he could pursue anything with Natalie. The veritable two ships in the night.

He hadn't been able to stop thinking of her since.

Turning his attention back to his daughter, the flood narrowly averted, he held her hand as she hopped and skipped down the hall toward the kitchen.

"Daddy, why didn't the lady want her pretty lights turned on? She was mean at first, but then sad."

"She was, wasn't she? Hop on board and let's have lunch, sweetie." He hoisted her onto his shoulders and strode into the kitchen, ducking through the doorway. "You're right, she was kinda mean and sad, but she looked like she was sorry she wasn't nice to you. I bet you didn't know she's Uncle Calum's cousin, did you? The grandma lady next door was her real grandma."

Zach didn't think Belle was old enough to deal with an explanation of Nat losing her son, so he settled on reminding her not everyone was interested in decorating for the holiday.

"I know you want the neighborhood decorated for Christmas, but we won't bother her, okay?"

Belle leaned over and patted one cheek with her chubby hand. "Maybe we should just decorate her house for her? That would make her feel better."

Zach settled her in the captain's chair and quickly slapped together a PB&J. "Well sweetie, if she's really as sad as she looked, maybe she doesn't feel like having pretty decorations. Sometimes people just want to be left alone when they're sad. We'll give her another week or so. Then we'll see about going back and inviting her out for lunch or dinner."

That mischievous glint in her eyes set off his radar, knowing she was plotting instead of listening. "You don't go anywhere but in this house or backyard, right?"

She shot him her best innocent look, the glint not fading one iota, and said around a mouthful of peanut butter and jelly, "I know, daddy."

Positive he'd had the wool pulled over his gullible eyes, he let the matter drop. The more he went on about it, the more interested his little munchkin would be in getting that house decorated.

She was already hounding everyone else on the block to *decorate pretty-please—it was almost Christmas!* His little girl was independent and smart as a whip, but it came with a price. He had to watch her like a hawk.

Zach rinsed and put their dishes in the washer, then scooped Belle up from her chair. "Let's get you settled in your room with a book. Your favorite program will be on soon, and I need to get a few things done in my office before we can head to the park."

"Okay, Daddy. But I still think we should at least turn on the pretty lights next door."

Her guileless look didn't fool him for a minute.

"Absolutely not, Belle. We are *not* going to bother her, understood?" Zach pinned her with his *you better listen to me* look, turned and left the room to head back downstairs, swinging by the front door to check the deadbolt, set high enough to evade little fingers, to ensure he'd locked it. He'd already checked the back door, and the backyard was almost as secure as Fort Knox. He wasn't taking any chances with her safety.

After Zach settled into his office, he tried to concentrate and put Natalie out of his mind, to no avail. Her vulnerability, pretty face, and sexy body appealed to the purely male part of him, and her inner sweetness and kindness when she wasn't on the verge of losing her shit pulled at his hardened heart. He shook his head, determined to tamp down the attraction, like he'd done for the past couple of years. Been there, done that, had the loser's ribbon to prove it.

He needed to concentrate on his little girl's happiness and wellbeing, and try to suppress the protector genes running through his veins. And that damned attraction that came roaring back the minute he'd seen her face, and sexy, curvy body again.

But first, he was going to give Calum a ration of shit for not telling him Natalie was moving in next door. He pulled his phone from his pocket, swiped to unlock, tapped to see recent calls, and hit *Jock* to call his buddy.

❁ ❁ ❁

NATALIE COULDN'T turn off the waterworks now that they'd burst the dam of her control. She limped through the parlor into the hall as tears streamed down her face, almost mowing down the movers as they made their way out of the kitchen.

"Oh!" Fiercely scrubbing her wet cheeks, she peered at them through tear-spiked lashes. "I'm sorry. Ah, are you finished?"

They both fidgeted and looked anywhere but her face, the older man finally responding. "Yes ma'am, we're done. Do you need anything before we head out?"

"No, but just a sec."

She turned and limped back through the parlor, the men all but on her heels now that escape from the weepy female was possible. She reached into her purse to get their tip and extended her hand.

"Thank you so much for your hard work today."

She tucked the money into the bear-sized palm of the older, grizzled mover, then stepped back so they could make their escape.

The older man pulled open the door, turned and touched the brim of his hat in an old-fashioned gesture. He surprised her by looking her in the eyes, a kind twinkle in his. "I knew your grandma, miss. No finer woman to be found in our little town. I want to say how sorry I am for your loss. If there's anything you need, you just give us a call."

She stood frozen, dumfounded by his kind words and offer of help. Guilt crept in as she remembered her earlier, unkind thoughts that they couldn't wait to get away from her. If they knew her grandma, maybe she'd sensed worry, and they weren't being critical.

"Thank you for your help, and your offer."

She closed the door behind them and knew she'd really made a muddle of things. First with the movers, then with Zach and his daughter. She cringed, thinking about how she'd reacted to his little girl, snapping like a shrew at her. And what a shock to look up from that sweet tyke to see his handsome face glaring at her, before he realized who she was.

If she didn't watch it, she'd end up alienating everyone her first week back in town, and Zach nor his little one deserved her attitude. Her grandma had raised her to be stronger and kinder than that.

With a shake of her head, she entered the old kitchen, immeasurable comfort filling her to see nothing had changed since her last visit. Since her childhood, really. When she was little, the kitchen was where her grandma brought her for comfort.

She sighed. "A plate of warm, homemade peanut butter cookies and a cold glass of milk always seemed to make everything better, grandma. I sure do miss you."

"I loved those times with you, too, sweetie, and Lord do I miss you. But I'm not gone yet."

Natalie covered her cheek, where it felt like a soft kiss had dropped, her heart racing as she whipped around to see who'd spoken. Why, it sounded just like her grandma and felt just like when the older woman gave her an affectionate peck on the cheek! No, not possible. She didn't believe in ghosts or the afterlife, although Beacon Bay was famous for just that—along with magic. She was just missing her grandma so much she was imagining things.

Willing her heart to slow, she turned and picked up the old copper teakettle, the weight of it, along with those wonderful memories, a balm to her soul. Her grandma had believed the routine of preparing tea was settling. Natalie agreed.

The pain clawing at her heart finally reduced to a low, manageable hum. Her mind *finally* settled and her pulse slowed. She calmed enough to remember her cousin Calum had been expecting a call with her flight information that morning so he could pick her up. She'd just wanted to get settled by herself without him hovering, so she'd taken a cab.

He'll be worrying for sure, and I'll get one of his lectures for not calling. Calum in lecture mode was not a fun time.

Resigned to be scolded but good, she pulled her phone from her purse and scrolled to his name. It rang once, and she cringed when he lit right into her in lieu of a greeting.

"My spies say you're already at Grandma's house. You're going to re-injure your leg if you aren't careful. The only thing keeping you safe from my wrath is that I understand. I'm on my way over. Have tea ready."

Natalie, used to her cousin's autocratic ways, knew his bossiness was cover for the deep love he felt for her. She was also used to his deplorable phone manners, and wasn't the least bit surprised he'd hung up without letting her get a word in edge-wise or saying goodbye.

That was just Calum's way of ensuring she didn't dredge up excuses to keep him from arriving on her doorstep. He would insist on seeing with his own eyes she was truly holding up against the dark memories. Against the depression she'd fallen into after she'd lost Matty, and then again and again after each painful surgery.

When in truth? She felt *buried alive* by the depression. It just about crushed her—every damn day. She couldn't come to terms with her new reality. That after all this time, she was still alone, unable to recover from the agony of her empty arms.

Chapter Three

NATALIE SET HER phone on the sturdy oak table and dropped her face into her hands, knowing she had to get it together before Calum arrived. They'd grown up more like brother and sister than cousins, their Grandma raising them after they'd both lost their parents in freak accidents, just a few months apart, when they'd been twelve and thirteen. They'd leaned on each other during that heartbreaking time, and on their grandma. She'd been their rock. Their anchor in stormy emotional seas.

Nat had been there for Calum when, gravely injured overseas, they'd airlifted him to Landstuhl Regional Medical Center, next to the U.S. air base at Ramstein, Germany. That injury caused his early retirement from the Marines. He'd been MARSOC, as had Zach, now that she thought about it. Both were tough, honorable, brave, handsome men. Only what she felt for Zach was way at the other end of the spectrum than what she felt for her cousin.

Shrugging away the attraction she felt for the big man, she called Pie Town, famous for their pizza, and placed an order—hungry but definitely not up to fixing dinner for Calum or herself. At the peal of the doorbell, Natalie laid her phone on the counter, took a deep breath and made her way down the hall into the parlor. Calum's shadow darkened the entire stained-glass pane to the side of the door. It hadn't taken him long to walk the four blocks from his home.

She plastered on a smile she knew for a fact didn't reach her eyes and opened the door, arms spread wide. "Come give me a big hug and a kiss!"

A muscle ticked in his jaw as he looked her over before finally pinning her with worried, loving eyes. She knew what he saw. She'd lost weight. Was pale and couldn't ditch the dark half-moons under her eyes. She gave him points for not jumping right into scolding her.

He shook his head and strode into the house, closing the door behind him. She felt a sliver of peace as his lips brushed her cheek and he wrapped her in his burly arms. "You're in so much trouble, cousin."

Releasing her, he stepped back and fisted his hands on his hips, his glower hot enough to melt asphalt as his eyes drilled into her, the same gold-flecked, moss-green as her own.

Attempting to dodge his questions, she blurted out, "I have tea ready in the kitchen, and Pie Town should deliver your favorite soon."

"Trying to butter me up with food?"

Deftly moving around him, she hurried down the hall into the spacious old kitchen, her slight limp giving her away. She peeked over her shoulder and saw exasperation, worry, and an abundance of love written clearly on his expressive, dear face.

"At least wait until we're settled before you yell at me."

Her blatant ploy to disarm him had at least a fifty/fifty chance of working. He'd never been able to resist her cajoling, and she headed him off at the pass as she jumped right from the frying pan into the fire.

"I'm limping because I had surgery again, and I know you wish I'd told you, but there was nothing you could have done for me. You were so busy dealing with Grandma's passing and the funeral. You didn't need to be worrying about me too."

Calum cursed and shot her a look of exasperation. "I knew your excuses for not coming out after she passed were feeble, that there was no way you'd have willingly missed her funeral. I should have flown out there to find out what you were up to."

His frown could have peeled paint, and Natalie realized she wasn't off the hook yet. They'd always been truthful with each other. She'd hated lying to him before, and just couldn't bring herself to lie to him now.

"Truth? I couldn't handle it. Couldn't handle your sympathy if you came to help. Losing Grandma the day after another surgery was too much."

She'd fallen and re-injured her leg a week before her grandma died, on the third anniversary of Matty's death, and had considered just giving up. She'd barely found the energy to go through another surgery and come out the other side in one piece emotionally and physically.

Her throat ached from the strain of holding back tears. She'd cried a river the past twenty-four hours, shocked there was any left. If she didn't get her act together and start living life again, her sadness and pain would consume her.

As she raised her eyes to his, she saw he understood far more than she'd given him credit for. "Her death, the surgery, the third anniversary and Christmas looming brought it all back, fresh. As if it had happened right then. Calum, I was so close to losing it. To losing my mind, like I did just after losing Matty."

Calum rose, ignoring Nat's raised hand, and went to one knee by her side, engulfing her in his familiar, comforting arms. She buried her face in his shoulder and a torrent of tears unleashed as he patted her back gently. "Nat, it'll be okay, I swear."

Her head felt like it weighed a ton when she raised shimmering eyes to his. "I'm sorry. I promised myself no more tears, and that I wouldn't fall apart on you."

Guilt bit at her at the thought of how she'd snapped at Zach's little girl earlier in the day. "I thought I'd be okay, but almost had a panic attack on the porch earlier. I'd just pulled out of it when a little girl came up the steps. She reminded me so much of Matty. Same age, same size, same chocolate-brown eyes."

Her gaze dropped to her clenched hands. "I was horrible to her, and it was Zach's daughter. I must have hurt her feelings so badly. She just asked about turning on the Christmas lights, and I snapped at her. Why didn't you tell me he lived next door?"

"I'm sure it'll be fine, and I honestly didn't even think to mention it when we talked about you moving back here. You'd met him just that once, at the hospital, right?"

"Well, yes, but we spent the better part of an entire week together. He was nice to me back then—we became friends of a sort—and maybe I could have prepared myself to see him again, and not been mean to his daughter."

"I swear, he'll understand, especially once he knows you're coping with recovering from surgery, and he already knows about Grandma's passing. I didn't tell him you were moving in, either. He remembered you, didn't he? Besides, he's not the type to hold a grudge."

She rose and turned around to grab the teapot. "Yes, he remembered me. After he shot daggers at me. He was very protective of his daughter. Not that I blame him. I would have acted the same way."

Nat shook her head at him when he reached for her, swiping a stray tear from her cheek. "It was embarrassing, and when he tried to find out what upset me, I ducked into the house and slammed the door in his face. Oh, never mind, I'll just stay away from him, and his daughter."

She shot him a mutinous look and changed the subject. "I need you to help me with PT again. The reason I had another operation is that I tripped and fell down some stairs a week before we lost Grandma. The fibula was already weak from the previous injury and surgeries, and a new hairline fracture appeared. They had to put in a small rod."

"Why didn't you call me when you fell?"

She squirmed before meeting his hard gaze again. "Wasn't a darned thing you could do. You'd missed enough work during my previous surgeries. I didn't want to bother you, and then grandma died, and no way was I going to worry you while you were coping with that. I'm just sorry you had to deal with the funeral and everything by yourself."

"That's bullshit, Nat, and you know it! I make my own hours and can afford to take time off. What's really going on here? It's like you'll do anything to sabotage getting better and being happy."

She slapped her hands on the table and shouted back. "I don't deserve to get better or be happy! I let my child die!"

Chapter Four

ZACH KNEW IT was wrong to pull a Peeping-Tom on Calum and his cousin, but he couldn't drag his eyes away, even as guilt bit at him for spying on them. Belle was down for a nap and he'd taken trash out to the can. Which just happened to be across from Natalie's kitchen window—currently open several inches, along with the curtain.

He couldn't believe it when his buddy had admitted during their phone call that Calum's own cousin was his new neighbor. He knew the house had belonged to Calum's grandma. Heck he and Belle used to visit with the older woman, eating cookies and enjoying stories about Cal and Natalie when they were kids.

Why his buddy had felt the need to keep Natalie a secret, he had no clue. Calum had plenty of opportunity in the past few weeks to mention who Zach's new neighbor was going to be. It caught him by surprise she turned out to be the pretty cousin his buddy had mentioned a few times when they'd served together overseas, and he'd finally met during Cal's stay in the hospital a couple years ago.

He stood frozen to the spot, and his chest tightened when he heard her tell Calum about her surgery—about how her grandma's death had devastated her. And losing Matty. God, he couldn't imagine recovering from the loss of a child. He'd heard the bare-bones of the story from Cal just after it had happened, and their grandma had mentioned it, too.

He couldn't pull away, even when she collapsed in tears and Cal folded her in his arms, rocking her like she was a child. For a crazy moment, he wished *his* arms were enfolding her. *No!* No way was he getting involved in their business. He didn't have the time or inclination to get involved with anyone. Even if the attraction that had hit in Germany had never waned, and she'd popped into his thoughts—frequently—since he'd met her in person. Belle was his focus. His *only* focus.

He strained to hear, but only snatches of conversation floated across the fence. He leaned against the rough boards when she mentioned his daughter. *Belle reminded her of Matty?* A shiver ran down his spine. Awww, hell. That's right, her son had been Belle's age when she'd lost him.

The pain and remorse in her voice cut like blades and he felt his resolve to remain detached slip away. She said she understood his protectiveness, that she would have been the same with Matty.

Three surgeries, man oh man. What she'd been through would've beaten down the average person. Then her grandma had died. On top of losing a child, and then having Belle appear out of nowhere. No wonder she had a precarious hold on her emotions. Too much pain on top of loss, moving, and recovering from surgery. Not to mention the holiday looming.

Zach rubbed a tired hand down his face and stiffened when Calum shouted at her. He wanted to run over and tell him to lay the hell off. He froze when she shouted back, "I don't deserve to be happy! I let my child die!"

Zach jerked away from the fence, strode to his back door, and stomped into the house. He didn't believe for a minute her child's death was her fault. He didn't know everything about her, but in his gut knew she wasn't responsible. Not after all the stories Calum had shared about her, and having spent that week in close quarters together.

Survivor's guilt was a bitch. He'd battened it back after getting out of the service. Had fought it and won—and had the scars on his heart to prove it.

No way was he getting involved, though, trying to shore up his resolve again. He'd hung up his knight-in-shining-armor suit years ago. It had never brought him anything but grief. Besides, he had his hands full working and taking care of his daughter.

He didn't have time for a normal relationship, much less one with someone carrying around all that emotional and physical baggage. Nope, no way.

If Calum thought to suck him in by not telling him who was moving in next door, he had another think coming. Besides, it was apparent she wanted nothing to do with him or with Belle.

Fine by him. He wanted nothing to do with her. If he could just convince his munchkin to leave the woman alone, they could continue with their separate lives.

Now to convince his unruly libido, and his lonely heart, she was off limits, too.

❅ ❅ ❅

CALUM JUMPED to his feet. "For the love of God, Nat! You didn't kill Matty."

She cringed when Calum shouted at her. Her own avenging angel. She hated to upset him, but he couldn't ever convince her she wasn't to blame. Her son had depended on her to keep him safe. To keep the monsters at bay. Especially the monster who'd once vowed to love and protect him. Her child's own father.

She'd failed, miserably.

"Enough, Calum. I just can't do this with you right now."

Her insides quivered with the need to huddle in a dark room, the covers pulled over her head. For about a hundred years.

Saved by the bell, literally—the welcome jangle of the doorbell heralded dinner's arrival. Guilt assailed her as Calum scrubbed a hand down his face in frustration.

Not up to answering the door, she turned to the cupboard to get plates and said over her shoulder, "Get the pizza please. I've already paid. You'll find tip money in my purse on the sideboard."

"Okay, Nat. You win. Today only, though. We're going to have a long talk soon about your misguided guilt."

She huffed out a breath as he strode from the kitchen, and thought maybe she should have stayed in Portland, where he couldn't bully her in person. Where she could just fade away until she burned out like a falling star.

Dinner was a tense affair, with her trying her best to keep the conversation light and flowing, and Cal unable to lose his glower and concern.

It relieved her to finally show him to the door, with a promise to make an appointment soon for PT, and to call if she needed anything.

Exhausted and in pain from moving, upset at herself for snapping at Zach's little girl, and out of sorts from the argument with Cal, she rinsed her after-dinner teacup, rose slowly from the table and limped the few feet to her bedroom.

God, she missed her little boy and her grandma. If it weren't for Calum, she'd wonder what the purpose was of even getting up to greet each day. She undressed and let her clothes stay where they fell, pulling on loose yoga pants and a skimpy tank before crawling under the covers, only to toss and turn into the night.

Nat groaned and glared at the numbers glowing neon next to her bed. Just shy of four in the fricking morning. She'd slept poorly, after finally falling asleep, in snatches of half hour or so.

The twinge of pain in her leg when she rolled onto her back brought a curse to her lips. She couldn't wait to get on with PT, and past this stage of healing.

"To heck with it," she whispered to the darkness. She'd grown accustomed to only a few hours' sleep at night. Not that she didn't crave a good night's sleep, she just felt she didn't deserve one.

What did it matter if she never walked without a limp again or was pain free? She didn't have anywhere she wanted to go. No one to visit. No child to run after. To play with. No husband, no lover. No. One.

She didn't need to be mobile in order to work. As a book editor, she could do her job sitting on her ass anywhere she chose. So what if she was tired of limping or having to use crutches? She had zero interest in doing anything, anyway.

A quick trip to the bathroom had her teeth brushed and her hair clipped into a messy knot on top of her head. She made her way into the kitchen, thinking that sleeping in the cozy room was a comfort, making her feel closer to her grandma, who'd slept there in her later years.

Originally the maid's quarters, it was a large airy suite, complete with its own bathroom. It was perfect for her needs. No way could she be up and down the stairs more than once a day until her knee and shin strengthened.

With the kettle full of water on the stove to heat, she put fragrant fusion green mixed with Earl Grey tea leaves in a diffuser, and into the pot. A couple of strong cups would banish the cobwebs in her brain, at least for a few hours. Maybe a nap in the afternoon would help.

She'd been putting off getting back to work, but in a week she'd need to get on it, or she'd disappoint the author whose book she was due to edit. No way would she do that to her valued clients, or damage her reputation by being unreliable. If she didn't start it soon, though, she'd be working day and night to get it done by deadline.

She had to get it together this morning, so she could get at least a few boxes unpacked before heading to Calum's for PT later that afternoon. Resigned to getting her shit together, she poured boiling water in the pretty sunflower teapot, grabbed the matching cup, and set it along with honey and a raspberry scone on a tray.

She pulled scissors from a drawer, added that to the tray, and limped into the parlor. A sigh escaped at the sight of the boxes lining the walls. She would unpack just enough to get through the next few days, and worry about the rest over the weekend.

Just the thought of PT made her tense up, remembering how painful her cousin's idea of therapy was. Not wanting to think about it, she set the tray on a pretty Queen Anne table and poured a cup of the fragrant brew. The first bracing sip had her feeling half-human again. The second was a welcome balm to her soul.

She hated being a shadow of who she used to be and was going to do something about it. Oh, she knew she'd railed at Calum about not deserving to be happy, but really, wasn't she diminishing the memory of her sweet little boy by refusing to live again? Who would share memories of him if not her?

She'd been kick-ass before losing her way, and it was high time she resurrected at least a part of the woman she'd been. If for no other reason than to celebrate Matty, even in death. Another sip of her tea, and she was ready to unpack boxes.

Natalie laid a flattened box on the growing stack in the room's corner, then groaned as she stretched. She was grungy, sore and tired, although she'd only been awake a few hours. She'd unpacked one entire wall of boxes, but had strained her back while babying her leg.

What an idiot, she thought. Thank goodness her PT appointment with Calum wasn't for another three hours. Plenty of time to get cleaned up and have lunch before heading down the street to his place.

Although she'd made great headway with unpacking, she hadn't been able to touch boxes with photos of

Matty, or keepsakes. She'd save those for a day she wasn't feeling so fragile.

"Sorry, little man. I'll get your pictures out later this week."

"You'll feel stronger soon, sweetie. There are folks here you can lean on, you know."

Natalie stumbled on the first stair step. She was either going crazy, or her grandma was haunting this house! She whipped her head around, of course seeing nothing.

"You're losing it, Nat. Hearing things. And what folks would I lean on? I have Callum, period."

Shaking her head, she made her way slowly upstairs to shower, and tried to convince herself she was imagining her grandma's voice because she missed her so much.

❄ ❄ ❄

ZACH TENSED, sensing he wasn't alone in his room, and cracked open one eye to see Belle not two inches from his face. Her eyes were drilling holes in him, with chubby cheeks sucked in until she had pursed fish lips.

Her method of silently willing him awake so he could make pancakes and fix hot chocolate was a little creepy, but she was like a sweet little fairy, flitting here and there, showering light on everything. He loved every one of her quirks to pieces.

Thank goodness he no longer jumped from his bed in readiness to defend himself when she crept into his room. It had taken a good six months to get to that point.

Countless times he'd scared the crap out of them both when he'd leapt from bed before realizing enemy combatants weren't crawling through his bedroom door.

He'd *finally* learned to ease awake when she gave him her 'I'm hungry, it's time to get up' laser stare.

"Hey pumpkin. How about you go get Mr. King and meet me in the kitchen?"

"Okay, Daddy. Mr. King wants banana pancakes!"

"He does, huh? Don't want to disappoint him. Do you think he'll get syrup in his mane again?" He remembered the past weekend when Belle had pretend-fed her stuffed lion. It had taken him thirty minutes to get the furry king cleaned up.

"Nope, he's gonna be berry careful."

Zach grinned and chucked her under her dimpled chin before she skipped out of his room. Every day was a miracle, in his opinion, since he'd foiled her mother's attempt to sell her for a week's worth of crack.

His thoughts turned murderous when he pictured the fate his little girl would have met if he hadn't found her. She'd all but forgotten the event, waking just once in a blue moon with nightmares—although still terrified of doorbells. She'd been three. Old enough to feel terror during the ordeal, but young enough the memories should fade away to nothing as years passed.

He swung his legs over the bed, fists clenched against his thighs. It was a good thing Jo Ann was in prison, locked away and no threat to Belle's safety or happiness. That day, when the bitch had taken his child, had been the first time since his separation from MARSOC he'd wanted to kill someone.

He'd have had no remorse either, and didn't know if he'd be able to control himself if they released her, and she attempted to see Belle. He *knew* he wouldn't be in control if she tried to kidnap her again.

While he slipped on sweatpants, his mind wandered to Natalie. He pictured her sexy body, and his heart gave a hard thump as he remembered his visceral reaction while watching through her window yesterday. Clearly emotionally devastated, he'd wanted her in his arms instead of Cal's. To be the one comforting her. Protecting her.

If his mind had wandered later in the night into fantasizing about how she'd feel naked and in the throes of passion, well, he'd just blame his long abstinence on that.

As he'd watched and listened through that kitchen window, something had snuck in and bypassed the protective wall he'd mortared around his heart—but he refused to succumb. He had Belle. By the skin of his teeth, his skills as Marine Special Forces, and his buddy Calum—he had Belle.

Besides, being a single dad took all his time. He had no time for an affair, much less anything resembling a relationship. So what if he was occasionally lonely and horny?

His head on straight and that wall around his heart shored up again, Zach jogged downstairs and into the kitchen. Belle was patiently awaiting her Mickey Mouse pancakes, with Mr. King holding court on the counter, looking less than ferocious decked out in one of her baby bibs.

"Who's ready for pancakes and hot chocolate? Looks like you protected Mr. King from sticky syrup this morning, eh, pumpkin?"

"He sure is, Daddy. He said he didn't really like his bath last weekend."

Zach swooped in and blew raspberries on her plump cheeks, reveling in her giggles.

"Mr. King wants raspberries, Daddy!"

He blew on the lion's furry face, eliciting hysterical giggles when fur fluttered and no sound emerged.

"Mr. King seems to be protected from raspberries, munchkin. Guess you'll get them all!"

After another raspberry and a pat on her head, he pulled the skillet, spatula, and pancake makings from the cupboards. He used cookie cutters to form different Disney characters with the batter, some resembling nothing more than an amoeba when he lifted the cutter too soon.

"Daddy? I was thinking."

He knew from the tone of her voice he was going to have to shoot down whatever she said.

"What, pumpkin?"

"Well, I know you said we shouldn't bother the lady next door, but I bet she needs help decorating. You know?"

"Belle. We talked about this yesterday. She doesn't want or need our help. I also found out that Uncle Calum is her cousin, so she has him to help her decorate. *If* she wants to."

"But, Daddy! Uncle Calum can't be there all the time. He works. But you work here and you're on vacation, right? So, if she needs help when he can't be there, we can help her!"

He turned to see her arms spread wide and a look of pure satisfaction light up her sweet face. Like she'd just solved a quantum physics problem and world hunger all in one—his munchkin had it all figured out. If she had her way, he'd do nothing for the day but decorate their new neighbor's house.

He felt a headache brewing. He'd spent a restless night thinking of Natalie every time he woke, about the pain of losing a child, about when he'd almost lost *his* child. As hard as he'd tried, he couldn't stop thinking about her too-thin, albeit sexy little body, either.

"Sweetpea, we will not bother her. That's final. I know you just want to help, but she's dealing with things right now. Things I don't think she wants to share with us." He couldn't tell Belle that she reminded Natalie of her dead child. That was too much information for a little girl to have.

"But, Daddyyyyyy. It's almost Christmas, and what if Uncle Calum doesn't have time to help her decorate? Or bake cookies? Or watch Christmas movies with?" She had a horrified look on her face by the time she stopped listing all of her must-do holiday activities.

"No, Belle. Stop your whining. She has Uncle Calum. She doesn't need us. You need to remember your promise from yesterday. You're to stay in the house or backyard. We're done talking about this right now. Why don't you go grab a book to read to Mr. King while I make the pancakes?"

If her mutinous look was any indication, the conversation was only on pause. To be resumed when she hit her internal play button. He made quick work of whipping up her favorite breakfast and got her settled, along with Mr. King, at the table. She placed the furry lion next to her where she could pretend to feed him, while Zach wolfed down his own stack.

He was due to drop Belle off at his sister's house for a girl's day, then head back home to get some work done in relative peace and quiet. Although on vacation, he still had blogs to write and other things to do. It did his heart good to know his sister and Belle loved their times together, with Randa a superb role model, who was also a fierce protector, and would let nothing happen to his little girl.

"Whoa, hold on, Mr. King doesn't want pancake syrup in his mane again." He'd looked up just in time to see Belle's fork, full of dripping pancake, making its way over to the king's furry mouth. No way did he have the time to spend another half hour cleaning stickiness out of that fur.

"But he said he's hungry, daddy."

"I'll feed him after I drop you off. A big, strong lion like that needs something more than just sweet pancakes, anyway."

Her sigh was as strong as a summer breeze, and he held back a chuckle.

"Okay, if you pwomise to feed him."

"Cross my heart, sweetpea."

Making quick work of cleaning sticky hands and cheeks, he bundled Belle into his truck, backed out of the driveway, and rolled slowly past Nat's house, his eyes inexorably drawn to the front windows, his view obscured by heavy drapes still drawn.

He sped up, turning onto Torch Drive and continued past Cal's house, then took a right onto Signal Street before turning into his sister's driveway, grinning to see her sprint out the front door waving madly.

She was a five-foot nothing curvy dynamo, with hair as black as his hanging down her back to her bottom, skin a shade darker like the silky feathers of a tawny owl, and eyes as stormy gray as his.

"Bellllllllle! Where's my girl?"

His grin widened to see Belle practically bouncing in her booster seat as Randa opened the door and jumped into the backseat, landing a smacking kiss on her chubby little cheek.

"Are you ready to have fun today, my sweet little miss? I have cookie dough ready to put in the oven, and some of our favorite shows ready to go!"

"Yay, Aunty Randa! Which ones?"

Belle bounced and cheered while Randa unbuckled her, her exuberance bringing happiness to his heart. His little girl didn't even give his sister a chance to answer before she launched into telling her about Nat.

"A lady lives next door, and she was mean to me but then sad and crying and knows Daddy and I think she'll feel better if she had her house decorated, don't you Aunty Randa?"

Zach gave an internal eye roll at his daughter's blatant attempt to get her aunt to side with her on the whole decorating the neighborhood campaign.

He stretched an arm across the back of the seat and waited for Warrioress Randa to appear.

"Who was mean to Belle? Someone you know was actually mean to my niece? Do I need to have a word with this woman?"

Zach gave a shake of his head and mouthed 'later' then said, "We just caught her at a bad time. I'll fill you in later. She's Cal's cousin."

Randa looked blank for a couple of seconds before her mouth rounded. "The woman who lost her, uh, well—the woman you mentioned you met when you returned from keeping watch over Calum in the hospital, when I was babysitting the little miss?"

It was Zach's turn to look blank. "When did I mention her?"

Randa smirked. "Oh, the night I brought the little miss home, and I convinced you to have a few shots to decompress. Remember? I stayed the night in case Belle needed anything, and you unloaded about how attracted you… uh, jeez. We need to talk when there aren't little ears everywhere."

"What's 'tracted mean, daddy?"

His little one listened way too closely, and thank goodness didn't understand half of what Randa just spewed.

"Later, Randa. We can chat later. Maybe tonight, when little miss britches is asleep."

"I'm not little miss bwitches! I'm Belle! Aunty Randa! We gotsta go bake cookies and paint our nails and watch the shows! Which ones did you pick?"

Randa shot him one more look that promised to pull all his secrets from him later, then turned back to Belle.

"I told you, little miss, your faves! I have Zootopia and The Snowy Day and Bino & Fino!"

"Yay! Bye daddy. Gotsta go! We have plans!"

Zach laughed and leaned over the seat to get smacking kisses on the cheek from Belle and Randa. He waved as they clambered from the vehicle, shut the door, and then both skipped up the sidewalk holding hands, right through the front door into the house, the door closing behind them.

As he backed out of the driveway and drove down the street, he hoped to heck he'd be able to tuck thoughts of Natalie back in the corner of his mind where she'd resided the past couple of years. Good luck with that, he thought. It would be a miracle if he got any work done.

When he turned off his sister's street and saw Natalie limping along the sidewalk, he cursed the universe for being against him, put on his signal, and pulled over.

Chapter Five

NATALIE GLANCED UP at the sound of a heavy vehicle door slamming shut, tripped over a crack in the sidewalk, and blinked in disbelief to see Zach practically leap across the curb and catch her before she could fall. He pivoted and sat heavily on the bus bench conveniently located to keep them both from landing on their butts on the cement, with her on his lap.

"Ooooof! How—where did you come from?" Natalie's voice was breathless as she peered up at him. She had no clue if it was from almost falling, being startled at seeing the object of her very thoughts before tripping, the solid feel of Zach's muscled quads under her bottom, or the bulging biceps circling her back and legs was responsible. She could feel his heart racing against her ribcage, and his voice was shaky when he answered.

"Just dropped Belle off at my sister's house and saw you on the sidewalk. Pulled over to offer you a ride.

Damn, Nat, you about shaved ten years off my life watching you fall. Where were you going? Don't you have a car?"

She blinked in confusion at his statement. Why would he care if she fell? Oh, she didn't think he was heartless and wouldn't feel sorry for her if she hurt herself again. But he seemed a tad more shaken up than just a neighbor or acquaintance would be. She dialed back into his questions.

"I have a PT appointment, and I sold my car when I left Portland. Can't decide what I want to buy, and Grandma's house—my house—is close enough to walk to Calum's. One of those online services delivers my groceries and other things."

"Well, I realize walking is probably good for your injury, and know you're aware of your limits, but I wish you'd consider letting me drive you to and from PT until you're a little steadier on your feet, if Cal can't."

The look in his eyes was one of concern, not one of those *'I know best, little woman'* expressions, which would have alienated her and raised red flags all over the place. The fact he waited for her to decide, with no impatience or irritation, also added to the growing list of things in his favor.

Not that she was keeping a list of pros and cons, no siree, but ever since her crazy bastard of an ex-husband went off the deep end years ago, she'd learned to categorize other's behaviors to determine if she should even give them the time of day, much less let them into her inner—tiny—circle of friends or even acquaintances.

So far, Zach was living up to the picture she'd formed years ago in Calum's hospital room of a compassionate, protective guy who would only lay the hurt on someone if they threatened anyone he cared about.

Realizing she'd sat there on those muscled quads for way too long staring up at the man, she stiffened and made to climb off his lap, only to realize she had nowhere to put her hands to accomplish that feat that wouldn't land in the wrong places.

"Uh, help me up, please."

She watched what seemed like reluctance flash through his beautiful, storm gray eyes before he stood and gently set her on her feet, keeping one big hand wrapped around her bicep to steady her. She sighed and told herself not to be a stubborn twit just because she was feeling emotionally fragile, and—she'd recently realized—was still enormously attracted to him.

That kernel of attraction that had popped up a couple of years ago had taken on a life of its own at seeing him yesterday, and was growing by leaps and bounds. Not good. Not good at all. But she could be adult about this, accept his offer of help—maybe redeem herself for snapping at his little girl—and get to and from Calum's without face planting, or winding up in surgery again. She'd spaced out, staring up at him, and when he opened his mouth, no doubt to offer again, she quickly spoke up.

"You're right. I'm not as steady on my feet as I thought I was, and certainly don't want to end up with another surgery. I'd appreciate it if you can drop me at Calum's."

Relief flashed through his eyes, and she realized how amazing it was to be around a man who showed his every emotion out there for her to see. This man would *not* surprise you with a hooded look and a fist to follow up. Not that Zach would ever hit her, she was sure of that. But she also wouldn't be caught off guard ever again with emotions that didn't match what she thought she saw on someone's face.

"Right, well, I'm happy to help out."

He kept his hand around her bicep as they walked across the sidewalk to his truck, and it remained there as he opened the door with his other hand, before he released her to wrap his powerful hands around her waist and lift her effortlessly into his truck.

She cringed at the squeak that emitted from her throat, but to be lifted so effortlessly when she wasn't expecting it would make anyone exclaim. She knew she'd lost weight, but she was no featherweight.

Those biceps weren't just for show, she thought with a silent sigh of admiration she quickly tried to squelch. She barely had the emotional or physical energy to take care of herself, much less the energy to offer anyone any kind of relationship. Well, except maybe as a friend she kept at arm's length. *Maybe* she could manage that.

Her eyes tracked his athletic frame as he jogged around the front of the truck, opened the driver's door, and climbed inside. He shot her a quick glance before starting the engine, looking ahead and behind, then executing a U-turn to head back the way he came, toward Calum's gym.

"Thanks for letting me help you out."

His deep voice broadcast his sincerity, and Nat had to shore up her resolve to keep him firmly in the *casual friend* zone.

"You're welcome."

They made the quick drive two-blocks to Calum's, and Zach reversed his actions before she could even get her door open, clasping her bicep again, then helping her ease to the ground.

They both swiveled their heads at Calum's shout, "What happened?"

Nat grasped Zach's forearm to ask him not to tell Cal she'd almost fallen. She didn't want to endure another lecture, even if it was well-meaning and from a core of love. She was surprised and grateful when Zach reassured her cousin without lying or giving away her near-miss.

"Nothing, bro. Nat accepted my offer of a ride to PT, since I was out and about anyway, dropping Belle off at Randa's."

Natalie turned back to Zach and mouthed, "Thank you," mesmerized by the heat that flashed through his eyes as they locked on her lips, before his gaze roamed across her face before finally pinning her eyes with his.

Fascinated to see him shake his head before stepping back, then turning with her next to him to face Calum, it was all she could do to tear her gaze away from his handsome face and unlock her voice.

"Well, thanks again for the ride, Zach."

"You're welcome. I'll be back in, what, an hour to pick you up?"

"Oh, no, you don't need to come back. Maybe Calum, or an Uber…" When Zach just shook his head, and Calum spoke up, she trailed off.

Calum looked apologetic when he said, "Can't today, Nat. I have another client right after you're done."

Zach ghosted a fingertip down her bare arm, giving her chills that had nothing to do with being cold. The opposite, in fact.

"You never know what size car will pick you up with those transportation companies. I don't think your leg can cope with being cramped, can it?"

Natalie curbed a sigh before caving and responding. "No, probably not. I'll be ready in an hour, and would appreciate a ride home." She suddenly wondered if his daughter would be with him when he came back for her. She didn't think she could cope with that.

"Will…" She hesitated, not wanting to offend him, and also not wanting him to ask why she was asking, so came up with as innocuous a question as she could. "Will this interfere with you picking up your daughter?"

She caught the keen look in his eyes and realized he must have spoken to Calum about her at some point in the past few years. Maybe even since yesterday. There was no pulling the wool over this guy's eyes.

"Nope, she's spending the entire day with Randa—Miranda, my sister—and she'll drop her off this evening after dinnertime."

"Oh, well, in that case, if you really don't mind, an hour from now is great."

With a chin lift for her cousin, and a look she couldn't decipher for her, Zach gave a wave and a "later", pivoted and headed around his truck again to climb in and drive off, Natalie unable to take her eyes off him until he was down the street.

"Hey, now that he's gone, how about you tell me what's really going on, and if there's any new damage we need to work on?"

She whipped her head around, realizing she'd been so caught up in thoughts of Zach and watching him leave, she'd all but forgotten her cousin was still standing there. A blush crept up her neck and across her face when she realized her bossy cousin could still read her like a book, and know when she was stretching the truth, or perhaps not being fully transparent about something.

He'd had that uncanny ability when they were children growing up together, and she should have known he'd only sharpen that knack as an adult.

"Fine, you'll torture me with questions until I tell you, so I may as well get it over with. I was walking here for my appointment, slowly and carefully, and Zach pulled over to see if he could give me a ride. He startled me and I started to fall. Since he apparently has lightning-fast reflexes, just like you, he scooped me up before I landed on my butt and then gave me a ride. Happy now?"

She hated how snippy she sounded, but just had no steam left and wanted to get PT out of the way, then ensconce herself back home in her grandma's house, away from sympathetic eyes and questions about how she was doing.

Worn out, both physically and emotionally, and on a fast track to becoming a hermit, *that's* how she was doing. And there was nothing anyone could say or do to stop her slow slide into depression.

❄ ❄ ❄

ZACH RUBBED a hand down his face and leaned back in his office chair, lecturing himself to stay emotionally detached from Natalie, while also being there for her if she needed him. His protector genes were roaring to the forefront, not to mention that blasted attraction he'd felt for her ever since their time together in Cal's hospital room.

He'd been working non-stop for the fifty minutes after dropping her off at Cal's and needed to get back there to pick her up so she didn't wonder if he'd forgotten her.

"Damn, what is it about her?"

"She's sweet, loyal, independent, and pretty to boot. What's not to like?"

Zach whipped his head around and took in his empty office, fully expecting to see Nat's grandma standing there, imparting wisdom and attempting to steer him in the right direction whenever he started to go off course—like she had when she was alive.

"What the hell?" He glanced around and wondered if lack of sleep and worry were getting to him. He'd slept for shit last night, thoughts of the pretty Natalie filling his head, along with worry about her apparent injury and weight loss vying for attention.

"Gram Edna, no haunting allowed."

He felt foolish, scolding a dead woman, but hell, if that hadn't been her revisiting him, then he really was losing his mind. He stood and stretched, grabbed his keys off the desk, then strode downstairs and out the front door, soft feminine laughter floating down the stairs after him.

He pressed the button to unlock his truck, opened the door, and slammed it closed, shaking his head in disbelief. He'd heard rumors about their being magic and hauntings in Beacon Bay, but hadn't put much stock in it. Granted, he'd only been living here a few months, but still. Magic?

Vowing to ignore any grandmotherly advice from beyond the grave, and to keep his heart locked away, he drove the short distance to Cal's clinic, pulled into the pickup zone in front and decamped the vehicle in time to see Nat exiting the building, Cal a shadow in the doorway, a scowl on his face.

Wondering if the cousins were arguing, he gave his buddy a chin lift, opened the passenger door for Nat and cupped her elbow as she put a shapely leg on the running board, then clutched the oh-shit bar to hoist herself in.

Unable to just stand there and watch her struggle, he wrapped both hands around her trim waist and gave her a boost, wondering at the blush that swept across her pretty face when she got settled.

"Everything okay?"

With a soft sigh, she shot a quick glance his way before looking out the windshield again. "Yes, Cal's just not happy with my lack of progress since the surgery."

"Was it recent, the surgery?"

"The day before—before grandma died."

He had to lean in to hear the rest.

"That's why I didn't attend the funeral."

"Aw, sweetheart." He shook his head. Afraid to say too much, and unable to stay quiet. "You've had a rough time of it. Let's get you home, uh, to your house and settled."

He gave himself a hard, virtual kick in the ass at the Freudian slip; the thought of taking her home and getting her settled in *his* house a little too appealing for comfort.

Rounding the front of the vehicle, he climbed in, pressed the starter button and pulled away from the curb. Abandoning all self-preservation of his heart, he glanced her way and asked, "You must be hungry after Cal's torture session. Want to stop for a bite, or get something to go?"

His peripheral vision caught her head whipping toward him before she turned front again, and he almost held his breath, waiting for her response.

"Uh, well."

He waited patiently, afraid anything he said would tip her decision to go home alone.

"I'm kind of sweaty, and don't really feel like eating in a restaurant."

Well, he thought, that wasn't an all-out *no* to lunch.

"Okay, how about I swing into the drive thru for Kurt's Crab Shack? With his variety, we should both find something we want." Hoping to elicit a smile from her, he teased, "Unless you don't like seafood. In which case, you better keep that a secret, being in a coastal town and all."

Her soft giggle was like winning the lotto, and he ignored his inner voice, asking why making her happy was so important to him—*if* in fact he was bound and determined to protect his heart and keep it locked away.

"I love seafood. Well, except for mussels and clams. But don't tell anyone I said that."

"Your secret's safe with me, Nat."

He glanced her way again to see another sweet blush sweep up her face and wondered what that was all about.

Once in the drive thru, idling next to the menu board, he about jumped out of his skin when she leaned over to read it, her hand resting on his bare forearm somehow translating in his brain to it being wrapped around that suddenly hard appendage between his legs. His heart suddenly racing, he dropped his other hand from the steering wheel down onto his lap to hide the fact he was hard as a pipe, just at the feel of her holding his arm.

It took all his willpower to continue looking at the menu, instead of turning his head to see how close her beautiful face was and possibly steal a kiss. Damn, why was his heart and libido suddenly in charge, instead of his brain? Had he felt this way for her the past couple of years without realizing it, and proximity was flipping all his switches to ON?

A squeeze on his arm and soft voice had him whipping his head around, and yup, sure enough, he was an inch away from her sensuous, full mouth. All he had to do was lean….

“Zach? You okay? Your turn to order.”

“What? Oh, yeah, uh, food. Right.”

His eyes dropped to those siren lips again, then back to her eyes, and her look of confusion transformed into one of understanding. That he was a hairsbreadth away from kissing the daylights out of her.

She jumped back as if poked with a stick, averting her gaze and waving at the menu.

He scrubbed a hand down his face, calluses scraping against the perpetual scruff on his jaws and chin before he faced the menu again and rattled off the first things that came to mind. As he pulled forward toward the window to pay, he realized it was a good thing he and Belle ate here frequently, since he had no clue what he'd just ordered.

All he could think of was the missed kiss, and when the next opportunity would be to see Natalie.

The young man at the window saved him from his impossible thoughts by handing across bags of food, which he passed to Nat. Drinks came next, and he pulled his wallet from the center console to pay.

“Oh! I didn't even think about having left my wallet at home when I said yes to stopping for food. I didn't mean for you to pay for my lunch.”

He turned and caught the embarrassed, uncomfortable look on her face and hastened to reassure her. “No worries, Nat. When I suggested it, I had every intention of treating you today. Consider it a welcome to Beacon Bay and the neighborhood."

He caught her sighing again and wondered if she was depressed or just exhausted. He knew sighing could be a sign of either.

"That's kind of you, especially considering how horrible I was to your—your little—to your daughter yesterday. I feel terrible about that, but…"

Zach pulled into the first available parking spot, put the vehicle into park and turned to face her, knowing they needed to get past this with the least amount of pain for her. He hesitated, then thought *to hell with it* before reaching for one of her hands to clasp in his, his thumb brushing across the top.

"Nat." When she kept her face averted, he gave her hand a little squeeze. "Natalie, sweetheart. No explanations are necessary."

That brought her eyes, swimming in tears, up to his. Oh man, this woman was in so much pain.

"Believe me when I say I understand. You don't need to explain, honest. Belle had shaken it off by the time she was scarfing her PB&J."

That got a watery laugh from her, thank god.

"And as for paying for your lunch, how about you buy me lunch later this week, or if you don't want to go out, if you want to just slap something together, invite me over for lunch. Randa keeps Belle for me on Tuesdays and Thursdays, so we can target one of those days."

At her look of gratitude, he felt about ten feet tall, when in fact he had done nothing to deserve that look. Anyone with half a heart would understand. Any man would want to spend time with her.

Was he setting himself up for heartache or happiness? If he kept them in the friend-zone, then neither of them would get hurt, and just maybe he could help her get acclimated to the area and provide an occasional ear and shoulder.

He just had to remember to not cross the line from friends to something more. Something hotter. Something with a life of its own. Especially since Belle was his focus, and Natalie wanted nothing to do with kids.

Dammit all to hell.

Chapter Six

NATALIE TURNED THE oven down to warm, having covered the lasagna so the top wouldn't dry out. She wondered if she was a crazy woman, inviting Zach over for lunch. It was Tuesday, and his daughter would be at his sisters, so she wouldn't have to worry about the waterworks turning on when interacting with her.

It has been two weeks since he'd rescued her from falling on the sidewalk while walking to Calum's gym, and they were both fooling themselves into thinking they were successfully ignoring the darned attraction that apparently had started all the way back in Cal's hospital room.

She'd had no clue, too damaged at the time to recognize it for what it was. It had only been a few months since her ex-husband's betrayal and loss of the most important part of her life. A piece of her heart had died that night, and she'd been hoping the rest of her would just follow along.

Refusing to go down that thought path, she turned and surveyed the kitchen, wanting to present a warm, comfortable lunch experience without it appearing romantic. Should she have used grandma's better dishes? Should she have dressed better, or more casually?

Gah! It had been years since she'd entertained a man and apparently had no clue what to do anymore.

"Stop fretting, sweet girl, and just enjoy that man's attention."

Natalie didn't whip around like she'd done the first time—or the tenth time—she'd heard her grandma's voice. Still not convinced she wasn't losing her mind, a part of her felt comforted at the thought her grandma was hanging around to make sure she was settling in.

Although, if there was life after death, why couldn't she see her little one, at least one more time?

She stifled a sob and straightened her shoulders, determined not to be a weepy woman when Zach arrived. He'd been patient with her silence, and with her refusal to have anything to do with Belle. She just wasn't ready to interact with a child the same age Matty had been when she'd lost him. Didn't mean she'd always feel this way, but for now, it was the only way to cope.

"Grandma, if you're really sticking around, and my mind isn't going, thank you for everything, and I'm sorry I wasn't here for you when you died."

She didn't even jump at the fleeting feel of a kiss on her forehead or pat on her shoulder before the room felt empty again. A smile lit her face, thinking how fitting that the spirit of her grandma would find a way to be here with her, considering how kick-ass and strong willed she was in the flesh.

The peal of the doorbell had her swiveling and making her way carefully to the front door, not wanting to undo any of the good her cousin had done in recovering some of her mobility. That small voice in the back of her head telling her she was getting too close to her handsome, kind neighbor was ruthlessly shoved into a corner of her mind and locked away.

They were both adults and could maintain a friendship without crossing the line, and she didn't want to lose this foray into normalcy he was providing. And if her libido had woken a little, too? Well, she could ignore it, just like she'd done for the past few years, even before she'd sent her ex to prison.

She peeked through the clear portion of the stained-glass panel to the side of the door, her heart tripping at the sight of all that muscular perfection standing tall on the porch. A twist of the lock and knob had the door opening, and the sexy smile that curved those masculine lips had her squelching a sigh.

Apparently, today would be another attempt at hiding her attraction from this big man, who apparently could trigger every erogenous zone on her body by just gazing at her with those smoky gray eyes, along with the smile that said he was happy to see her.

"Come on in, lunch is ready and warming in the oven."

"Oh man, you made lasagna, didn't you? Is that your grandma's recipe? She made it for us a couple of times and let me tell you, it was the best I'd ever tasted."

"I'm glad you enjoyed it. Now get in there and enjoy my granddaughter, too."

Zach and Nat swiveled their heads in unison, eyes wide, before turning to stare at each other, neither apparently ready to admit they'd heard something.

Zach recovered first, rubbing a hand on the back of his neck before scraping it across his face. "Did." He stopped, looked around again, turned to stare at Natalie, then started speaking again. "Did you, uh, hear anything just then? I have to admit, I've kinda thought I've been going a little crazy, but—if you—well, did you hear something?"

Natalie gasped and grabbed his arm, glanced around again, and whispered loudly, "Did you hear grandma? I'm not going crazy?"

Soft laughter trailed from the room and up the stairs as they both stood stock still, looking at the stairs as if watching someone climb them.

Zach chuckled, took her hand from his arm and linked their fingers before leading her into the kitchen, having been there when Grandma Edna was alive, and again when Nat had invited him for lunch a few times in the past couple of weeks.

"You're not going crazy, Nat, but I've gotta tell you the past couple of weeks I've thought I was losing it. I've heard her several times, mainly when I've been talking to myself."

"Holy shit, I was sure I'd finally lost it and was hearing voices because I miss her so much. And because I felt so guilty for not being here when she died, and then missing her funeral."

Zach hadn't crossed the line of more than hand-holding, or carrying her that one time she'd almost fallen, so when he wrapped those muscular arms around her and tugged her against his massive pecs, enfolding her as if shutting out the world and anything that could hurt or upset her, she simply froze, then melted against him like butter in the hot sun.

"Aww, sweetheart. You know your grandma would understand and wasn't one to hold a grudge. She also knew how much you loved her and appreciated her. I can't tell you the number of stories she told us about you, and Cal, and how often she expressed concern for you or reminisced about the good times you three had when you and Cal lived with her."

Suddenly torn between crying her eyes out, or tearing his clothes off, Nat decided to just wrap her arms around him and stay in the circle of his arms. Apart from his rocking body, his compassion was sexy, too. Where were these out-of-control emotions coming from? After her heart being dead for so long, she wasn't sure what to do with this wild desire.

She stifled a sob, and her traitorous body snuggled closer when his arms tightened around her. Was it wrong to want some comfort from someone not her cousin? From a man showing every sign of being as attracted to her as she was to him?

Or was she misunderstanding attraction for sympathy and comfort? Her answer came in the form of what felt like a steel rod pressing against her tummy before Zach jerked his hips back a hair. Her breasts were still pillowed against those magnificent pecs, but he was careful to keep that stiff, apparently just-as-excited-as-her part of him from nudging her tummy.

Welp, that answered her question. Not that she thought either of them would do anything about it. Nope, he had a young daughter she still couldn't bring herself to meet or be around, and she had so much baggage she almost needed to rent a storage unit to fit it all in.

A mirthless laugh almost escaped at that thought, and Zach, darn his ability to tune in to her moods, spoke up.

"You okay, sweetheart?"

She reluctantly pushed away, and he seemed just as reluctant to let her go. "I have no clue why you want to spend any time with me. I was just thinking I need a self-storage unit to handle all this emotional baggage I keep carrying around. Why would you want to deal with me? With it? There are so many other women out there, more attractive and less damaged than me."

"Hey. Baggage aside—because believe me, I have some of my own—we're just two adults enjoying each other's company. And I do enjoy yours, beautiful lady. Doesn't need to be any more complex than that. Belle's mother burned me before and after she was born, and I gotta tell you, my heart locked itself down afterwards. I don't think either of us is looking for anything more right now, yeah?"

A quick glance at his face showed nothing but sincerity and honesty, along with the banked fire in his eyes. Okay, they were in agreement, then. She would just enjoy his company, no pressure, and keep her heart tucked away, too. So what if the thought of holding their relationship at friends-only made her heart give an unhappy thump in response?

They both jerked their heads toward the ceiling when a ghostly *harrumph,* along with the sound of a door slamming, echoed from upstairs.

When their eyes met again, they shook their heads in unison and turned toward the kitchen.

"Grandma never was afraid to let me know when I'd disappointed or annoyed her." Nat glanced toward the ceiling again before pushing open the swinging door and entering the kitchen.

"When I was overseas with Cal, there were times we'd both swear we were in the presence of ghosts. There was so much death and destruction, and so many areas we were in were ancient. I'd see apparitions out of the corner of my eye, hear crying, mumbling, and outright yelling, when there was no one but us two in the area. But I've gotta say, this is my first encounter here in the United States."

She turned, pulled out a chair, and sat. "I've never seen or heard a ghost until Gram, although you must have heard about how magical Beacon Bay is, from all the way back when it was settled?"

"Yes, I've heard some stories, but thought they were just legends and not necessarily based in reality."

Zach walked around the table and stopped at the stove, pulling open the door and donning the potholder gloves. She idly wondered how they could possibly fit those broad palms and thick fingers, and then immediately got sidetracked, wondering what those hands and fingers would feel like on her bare skin, strategically placed for maximum pleasure.

Something of what she was thinking must have been apparent, because Zach stopped what he was doing and swept his gaze from her flushed face, down her body like a caress before making his way back to her now flaming cheeks.

His voice so soft and raspy, she had to lean forward to hear him. "Want to tell me what put that look in your eyes, on your face with that sexy flush to it?"

She now knew just what the term *deer in the headlights* meant. "Uh, well. Nope, you just keep doing what you were doing and ignore me."

He gave her another heated look before turning to pull the lasagna from the oven, and she wondered if she heard him correctly when he muttered, "Fat chance I can ignore that sexy body and beautiful face."

His comments took her by surprise, since she was feeling anything but sexy or beautiful. Choosing to ignore what he said, she realized she was letting him play host when she was the one who'd invited him over for lunch. "Oh! Here, just set that in the middle of the table on this big trivet, and I'll get our drinks."

Jumping up, she opened the fridge and leaned over to peruse the shelves. "I have local beer from Bonfire Brewery, cola, iced tea and water."

She turned her head just in time to catch his eyes on her ass, and realized bending over like this, in tights and a tunic that had risen, presented him with quite an eyeful. A slight turn of her body provided a profile view to him, and her butt was no longer front and center.

Now it was his turn to blush, his face turning a dull red as he turned and set the pan on the hotplate as directed. "I'll take a beer."

"I, uh, have several. Fyre Spice, Baken Honey, and Lodestar Dark."

She turned to see him leaning against the table, arms crossed against that massive chest with biceps bulging. Argh! How was she supposed to stay firmly on this side of the friend zone when all she could think of was getting him naked in her bed? Especially with that heat brewing in those storm gray eyes, like a tornado crossing the prairie ready to sweep her up.

He pushed off the table and crossed the room to lay a hand on the fridge door. "I'll take a Baken—Honey."

She grabbed the bottle, and an iced tea for herself, then squinted at him as she handed it off, wondering at the pause before he'd said honey. It sounded almost like an endearment. Like a caress across her senses.

Choosing to ignore every wayward thought she was having today, she shut the door, walked around him, and sat at the table. She could play it cool as a cucumber. What other choice did she have? He deserved more than half a heart, and considering she barely had even that to offer, she needed to ignore any wild urges and remember how damaged she was.

If she hadn't been able to repair herself and pull out of the depression in all this time, what made her think she could do it now? Besides, he wasn't looking for a relationship, so she had nothing to worry about.

❁ ❁ ❁

ZACH HAD better start worrying about his inability to keep Nat firmly in the friend zone. Regardless how hard he tried, and how often he reminded himself she was not looking for a relationship—that she was emotionally bereft and didn't want to be near Belle—and would probably never even consider being part of a family again, his damned heart and libido refused to fall in line.

It wasn't just her looks, her beauty, and her sexy body, though. She had a kind, beautiful soul and personality, to go along with her physical beauty and rockin' body. She'd started putting on weight and muscle tone just in the few weeks she'd been working with Cal, and her skin and hair had taken on a healthy glow and sheen, too.

They had established an odd sort of friendship, keeping their conversations light and dodging anything having to do with her son, Belle, or her grandma. Shew! He had no idea how someone ever got over the loss of a child, especially when they felt some responsibility, even if it wasn't the least bit her fault.

He figured he'd feel the same guilt, though, regardless of the circumstances. A caring, loving parent felt it was up to them to protect their kids, and no matter what tore that child away, they would always feel guilt to some degree.

So why was he foolish enough to keep seeing her? To keep offering to drive her to her PT appointments with

Cal? To continue taking her out to eat, or coming over here for lunch, although this was just the second time she'd cooked him a meal.

And what the heck was up with Grandma Edna haunting them? If he wasn't mistaken, the matchmaking busybody was trying to push him and Nat together. As much as he'd loved Edna—still loved the old woman—it wasn't going to happen.

"Hold your plate out and I'll dish the lasagna up. There's garlic bread, too, along with a veggie medley."

Her voice brought him out of the deep recesses of his mind, stopping the train speeding down the tracks of hoping for something more than mere friendship. A relationship, although he had no fucking clue how to be in one. Not a real, loving one, anyway.

He lifted and held his plate, admiring the play of muscles in her arms and the shadow of cleavage when she leaned over to put a generous spatula-full of noodle goodness on it.

With an inner groan, he surreptitiously adjusted his misbehaving cock, glad to have the table between them, and that he wasn't sitting next to her in a restaurant instead, where a glance at his lap would give him away.

Deciding he needed a distraction, he asked, "How's the editing going? Any interesting books this week?"

Her face became animated at his question, and he was glad to see he'd done at least one thing right today.

"Oh yes! A romance author I've edited one book for previously sent me the second in her series. It's a paranormal, bear shifter romance and wowza, can she write! Interesting plot, great characters and the sex, uh, well, she writes really well."

Zach grinned at her, realizing she'd been about to describe what great sex scenes the author had written.

The devil on his shoulder gave him a nudge he couldn't resist.

"Come on, Nat. Don't leave me hanging. What were you going to say? The sex…."

"Just you never mind, Zachary Esposito," she said primly.

"Oh, now you're just being mean. What's the author's name? Maybe I can pick up their first book and read it for myself?"

She looked equal parts horrified and intrigued, and he wondered if he would get insights into what sexy activities Nat enjoyed by paying attention to the sex in the book. Annnd, his cock would never go down enough for him to stand if he didn't stop thinking of sex and Nat naked. What the ever-loving hell was wrong with him lately?

"How's the web design and blogging business?"

Zach gave her a look, letting her know she was off the hook for now, before answering. "It's going well. A couple of my articles have gone viral, so I'll get good payout on those. I've also been uploading content on YouTube and TikTok, which is driving requests for articles and website design, so that's good. So far I've been able to keep up with the demand, but I have a couple of buddies I can refer folks to if I get too busy."

She beamed at him, and his traitorous heart gave another hard thump. "That's amazing! I'm glad you're staying busy. I know how important it is that you be able to work from home."

He realized she was always careful not to mention Belle, and he was savvy enough not to have hurt feelings, but still wished she was more comfortable with his situation at home.

"Yeah, I consider myself very fortunate to have business thriving." He grinned at her before saying, "I'm glad to hear you're enjoying the author you're working with. I still want to know her name."

"Sheesh, you're like a dog with a bone. Fine, her name is Dixie Dupret." She fiddled with her napkin, took a drink of her tea, and another bite of bread and wouldn't look at him.

"Thank you, Natalie," he said softly. Damn, he hadn't meant to embarrass her, and it seemed like he had by asking again.

"I'm sorry if I embarrassed you. That wasn't my intention. I would never hurt you—in any way. I hope you know that."

She lifted her head and nodded slowly, as if mulling over something. "I know that, Zach. And I'm fine, just being silly."

"Are we okay?" He may not be ready for a relationship, but he suddenly realized he did not want to lose this woman's company or friendship.

She looked startled for a moment, then gave him a shy smile. "Yes, we're okay."

He smiled in return. "Good. I don't want to lose your friendship, Nat."

She cocked her head at him before responding. "You won't."

Not ready to stay on a serious conversational track, he derailed that train and asked, "How's the PT going? I know Cal can be a hardass, uh, taskmaster when he's bent on getting someone back on their feet and strong again."

Her laughter showed she knew exactly what he was talking about. "It's going well, and he was that way as a kid, too! When he wanted something, boy was he single-minded and one-track. Whew! Has he helped you out in the past?"

Zach nodded ruefully. "Oh, yeah, before he even set up shop as a physical therapist. When we were overseas, I'd twisted my knee when running downhill with a full pack. Damn thing swelled up like a melon and hurt like hell. Cal ended up hoisting me over his shoulder, and another buddy grabbed my pack. By the time we got back to camp, I couldn't bend it or put any weight on it. After a week, the swelling reduced enough Cal started me on passive range of motion exercises, and it was another week before I could do the exercises myself."

She groaned in sympathy. "Oh yeah, and as careful as he is when he's manipulating the leg, it still hurts like hell, but he can harden himself and just keep doing it. I know it's necessary, but there were times I wanted to tell him to take a hike, get up and leave."

Zach nodded. "Yes! Exactly, except we can't get up and walk out, so we're stuck with the evil exercise master!"

"Ha! Yes! You totally understand."

It was the first time he'd ever seen her let loose with a full-bodied laugh, and it was an amazing thing to see. It mesmerized him, how her face lit up, the curve of her lips, dimples denting each cheek, and her head thrown back. She caught him staring when she opened her eyes and they widened. He had no clue what she saw in his expression, but he must have been broadcasting something she'd not seen before.

"What? Do I have red sauce on my face?" She wiped her mouth self-consciously.

"No sauce. You're just so fucking beautiful." He realized what had come out of his mouth when her eyes widened even more and her mouth dropped open.

Before she could toss him out on his ear, he held up his hands and backpedaled.

"Sorry, ignore me. I overstepped. What's for dessert?" He waited with bated breath for her to either give him the boot or serve sweets, and let out a relieved sigh when she merely gave him a considering look, rose from her chair and grabbed a covered dish from the counter, along with two small plates and forks.

"*About time you stepped up your game.*"

He ignored the ghostly whisper in his ear and internally rolled his eyes.

Who'd ever heard of a matchmaking grandma ghost?

Chapter Seven

IT HAD BEEN three weeks since Nat had served him lasagna for lunch. Three weeks of shared takeout meals in his truck on the way back from PT, but he'd received no more invitations to dine over at Casa Prescot. He had no one to blame but himself. Maybe if he hadn't blurted out how fucking beautiful she was, she'd be comfortable having him over.

At least she was still letting him ferry her around, thank god, but who knew how much longer that would last? When her leg was reliable and steady again, she'd probably be getting her own car and then he'd be obsolete, damn it all to hell. Probably catch a wave from her to and from their cars at most.

Grandma Edna still visited occasionally, but short of forcing his company on Nat, what was he supposed to do?

"How about inviting her over here? Randa can have an overnighter with sweet little Belle. And don't you worry, Nat will eventually open up to that little cherub. Who could resist?"

The pat on his cheek before the room warmed again told him Grandma Edna had flitted through just long enough to deliver her message. And it was a pretty good message, too. Somewhere between lasagna and when he'd woken this morning, he'd decided the attraction he felt for Natalie wasn't going away, and was in fact growing in strength and desire. That the kernel of affection in his heart was growing into something he as-yet refused to label.

If he really thought she didn't want him around, he would try valiantly to ignore it, except her actions convinced him she was just as attracted. That she also held some affection for him, and it was growing the more time they spent together. During the past week, he'd flipped from distrusting every woman on the planet and wanting to stay single, to wanting Natalie with every breath he took.

There may actually be something to the magic purported to swirl around Beacon Bay. He'd gone to the library over the past weekend and checked out a couple of history books written specifically about the magic and ghostly happenings.

The first folks who'd inhabited the area were Siuslaw First Nations, and they welcomed others to the area as they arrived, until it was a mix of different races and nationalities. Fascinated by the book, it had amazed him to learn about who all had arrived to make their homes here—mages, or magi, from Persia, druids from Ireland, fairy-folk from Scotland, Bruja from Spain, mediums, warlocks, witches, and wizards. The list had been endless and surprised the hell out of him.

Beacon Bay must truly have been a psychic beacon to magical folks, for such an eclectic mix to trek here, each and every person welcomed by the First Nations elders and healers. No wonder Grandma Edna was hanging around and sticking her ghostly, loving nose into their business. She somehow knew her granddaughter had been on a downward slide into deep depression, and also knew he had given up on women. The older woman still had work to do in Beacon Bay.

He'd spilled his guts to her one day, when Belle had been asking why other kids at school had moms who volunteered and loved them, and she didn't. Knowing she was too young to understand drug addiction and empty, evil souls, he'd hedged and said some people were missing love in their hearts, and that there were men and women who'd fathered and mothered children, but then were no longer in their lives.

Belle remembered how scared of her mother she'd been, so at least he didn't have to worry she'd go off with her willingly. He realized now, his stubbornness and distrust of all women because of one woman's perfidy and betrayal, and evil intentions, was ridiculous and robbing both him and Belle of the possibility of welcoming a loving woman into their lives. Especially with the realization Natalie may just be the woman for them.

Not to mention his little munchkin had been bugging him all week to meet Nat again, insistent that the sad expression she sometimes wore would go away if Nat just had bright Christmas lights and decorations at her house. And a little girl to read and talk to.

So far, he'd been successful in diverting her attention, but he knew his daughter was just biding her time, until she either wore him down, or somehow wheedled her way into actually talking to Nat, and wearing her down. He didn't think Nat was quite ready, and didn't want to alienate her before he even got out of the gate and started formally wooing her, even if she didn't realize it.

Thank goodness Belle hadn't out and out misbehaved and gone against his rules, but his little munchkin sure knew how to twist and turn them sometimes until you couldn't decide if you'd somehow agreed, or the rules didn't actually apply to what she was doing.

She'd make a brilliant attorney if she leaned that way as an adult. Until then, he just had to keep an eagle eye on her. Speaking of keeping an eye on her, he rose and strode from his office to ensure she was still in her room, where he'd settled her with coloring and puzzle books, and had turned on one of her favorite shows.

Then he would finish up and publish the blog he was writing, call Randa to see if she could keep Belle overnight on Saturday, and then try to convince Nat to come over for dinner. No, maybe he would invite both Nat and Cal, break the ice that way, then convince Cal to head home early.

If he wasn't mistaken, from the conversations he'd had with his buddy the past couple of weeks, he was fully on board with him pursuing Nat. Hopefully, with a ghostly grandmother and her cousin on his side, Natalie would eventually give in to their attraction, and he could add Belle into the mix. When she was ready. No way would he blindside her.

❄ ❄ ❄

BELLE KNEW she should color and watch *Dora the Explorer* while Daddy worked, but she couldn't stop thinking of the sad lady—Nat-alie—next door. She just knew that if the lady had colorful things to look at, like Christmas lights, she would be happier. Gram Edna used to tell her stories about Nat-alie, and Belle would wish she was her mommy. She still wished it, even though she was a meanyhead the other day.

Gram Edna had visited her just the other day. It had scared her enough to almost pee her pants at first, before she remembered hearing kids at school talk about friendly ghosts visiting them sometimes to help them out, or to say goodbye if they didn't have a chance before they died.

Two of the teachers were talking in the hallway, just outside her classroom door, about how Beacon Bay was a magical place and had ghosts visiting all the time. That it started a long time ago.

Gram Edna said something about Nat-alie having had a little boy, but he had died years ago and that was why she was sad—and why she was growly. Grammy said she thought Belle was just the thing her *sweet granddaughter needed.*

If that was right, then maybe she could run next door real quick like and plug in the Christmas lights, and Nat-alie would see that Belle wanted her to be happy. Daddy would understand after he saw how pretty they were, she was sure. After all, wasn't he always doing things to help the old people on their block? Although the lady next door wasn't old. She was pretty though, even when she was a mean grumpy-pants. But she hadn't been mean or grumpy since that first time, although Belle had only seen her through the window and not for real in person again.

After a quick trip to her room to tuck Mr. King into bed, she was tiptoeing out the back door, careful to close it quietly. She'd decided that through the small hole in the hedge between her backyard and Nat-alie's backyard was the best way to go, cause she wouldn't be breaking any promises not to leave the backyard.

Daddy didn't say don't leave their *backyard when he gave that rule, just not to leave* the *backyard. If the hedge wasn't there, then there would be just one big backyard!*

Belle was very proud of herself for figuring out a way to help decorate the house next door and obey Daddy's rules, too. She skipped across the grass, got to her knees at the small hole in the hedge, and wiggled and wormed her way into the lady's backyard, careful not to snag her t-shirt.

When she crawled out the other side, the old house towered above her. She missed visiting Gram Edna when she lived there. Belle had loved it when she would bake cookies and bring them over for her and daddy, or invite them over for a cookie party. She wished Nat-alie wanted a little girl to come over for cookies. And maybe a hug or two. Annnd, maybe read her a book, too.

She looked over her shoulder and wondered if her daddy was looking for her. Better be quick, before he found out she wasn't where he'd put her. She ran fast to the back of the house and stopped, the plug at the end of the Christmas lights laying at eye level on the porch just waiting for her.

❄ ❄ ❄

NATALIE HAD just finished yoga in the living room, having struggled through the entire session fantasizing about her handsome neighbor instead of regulating her breathing and concentrating on her poses.

She'd finished earlier in the day editing the second Dixie Dupret book and whew! That woman knew her sex scenes. Nat had spent so many years with her sexuality shut down, she wasn't quite sure what to do with her newfound libido.

She still had bouts of depression, still woke in a funk almost every morning, but found that as the day progressed, she could lose herself in the books she was working on, and more often than she wanted to admit, in thoughts of what Zach would look like sans clothes doing to her what was described between the pages.

He continued to ferry her to PT twice a week, although Cal said her leg was stable enough for her to drive again. She knew exactly why she was putting off purchasing a car. She'd lose her built in reason to see Zach, and would have to decide whether they could, or should, remain friends, taking meals together and becoming closer with every week, every day—every minute that ticked by.

It just wasn't fair to him, or to her, to keep up this charade, though. The one where he hoped she would want to be around Belle, and where she thought she still had a heart to offer that amazing man and his little girl.

She stifled a sob at the thought of not seeing him anymore, and of not holding a little chubby body in her arms, getting sticky hands caught in her hair, and slobbery kisses on her cheek. Oh man, what had she done? So what if she'd been sad, been unhappy all the time? Now she'd gotten a peek into what life could be like with Zach, with his little girl, and wanted it—but just couldn't risk it.

Couldn't go down that path again. Not that she thought he would ever turn out to be the evil bastard her ex had been. She didn't think Zach had it in him to even be mean without just cause. But her heart apparently didn't trust her brain, and the fear still had tight hold of her emotions.

God, she was such a fool! Fooling herself into thinking she could keep her feelings for the man superficial and ignore the fact he had such a sweet, motherless daughter. She needed her damned head examined.

What she needed to do was immerse herself in jasmine-scented water and soak her sore muscles. She'd overdone it today, between cleaning the house and too much yoga. The activity had kicked her ass, with her lower back in spasms and her leg aching to beat the band. The muscles on each side of her spine screamed for relief and a hot bath was just the ticket.

She needed to get her head on straight, and also needed to buy a car and let Zach know she wouldn't be needing a ride anymore, as painful as the thought of not seeing him, talking to him, sharing intimate meals with him was.

Grabbing her silk kimono, she carefully climbed the stairs to the bathroom on the second floor, that depressive funk threatening to overwhelm her again. The claw-foot tub in that room was cavernous and oh so comfortable. The once-a-day climb, just to sink into that sea of hot water, was worth it for the benefits to her damaged muscles and ligaments.

After entering and closing the door, she hung her robe on a hook on the wall, affixed her inflatable pillow to the slope of the tub, then adjusted the water to just-this-side of hot as Hades, adding a few drops of jasmine and eucalyptus oil. She needed to buy some lavender to help her relax. A groan escaped as she slid into the amazing heat, her back muscles singing hallelujah as she immersed herself.

A sigh slipped out as she lay back on the waterproof pillow and picked up her favorite paranormal romance book, unearthed from one of the many boxes she'd unpacked, determined to lose herself in the story and stop thinking of Zach, Belle, and her empty arms.

The soothing heat of the water was seductive, and Natalie's back was finally loose, her bones rubbery as a Halloween chicken. She set her book on the floor and sank fully into the water with a frown, the thought of how badly she'd treated Zach's little girl popping to the front of her mind again. He'd reassured her Belle was fine, with no ill effects of Nat snapping at her, but still.

Goodbye relaxation, hello guilt. She would be sure to speak kindly next time she saw her, *if* she saw her again, and not act like Scrooge McMeany.

Her eyes drifted closed as the warmth seduced her, coupled with her exhaustion from sleepless nights, and worry. Her last thought before sleep claimed her was how handsome and beguiling her new neighbor was, and how she wished she could be emotionally together enough to pursue the man.

Natalie's eyes popped open at the sound of her grandma's panicked voice. "*Wake up, sweetie! Get out of the house! Now!*" The rhythmic thumping and confusion over why she was sleeping in water made her muddle-headed.

"Grandma?"

She suddenly remembered her grandma was dead and gone as she looked around frantically, wondering at the strange noise. It amazed her she'd slept long enough for her candles to gut, leaving the acrid smell of smoke behind.

Water sloshed over the side of the tub when clarity roared to the front. She hadn't lit any candles! She looked around frantically and climbed stiffly from the tub, slipping on the book she'd set on the floor, her leg crumpling as it twisted. Shit, all she needed was a setback and to re-injure her leg!

The smell of smoke intensified, and she scrambled to her feet, realizing her damaged leg barely held her weight now, and snatched the silk robe from the hook.

"Oh my God, is the house on fire?"

Great, escaping with one good leg won't be easy. She jerked on the robe and lay a hand flat against the door. *Not hot.*

A yank had it opening, and she reeled back when a noxious cloud of smoke wafted around her head and snaked into the bathroom. She slammed the door and watched in horror as wisps of smoke slipped under it into the bathroom.

"Out the window, Nat, now!"

Heeding her grandma's instructions, she swiveled on her one sturdy leg and dunked a towel in the tub until it was soaked, then dragged it out and pressed it firmly across the bottom of the door.

Her eyes widened when she twisted toward the window, chest high and narrow. *How will I get out of that?* Good thing she'd lost weight the past few months, although she had put some back on, along with muscle.

The window creaked as she pushed it open and stuck her head out, relieved to see one of the fat branches from the old oak tree almost touching the side of the house. As she looked down, she wondered if she'd be able to climb out onto the tree without breaking her neck.

The thumping stopped the minute she slid the window open. A little shrieking voice had her glancing toward the back porch where a tear-streaked gamin face peered up at her. She was much too close to the flames licking at the porch and *holy shit,* what used to be her back door!

"You gots to get out of there, Nat-alie!"

"Get away from the house!" she shouted in panic. "Go home! Get your dad!"

Nat felt faint with relief to see the little girl scurry across the lawn and dart into a crevice in the hedge separating the houses. She could hear her screaming on the other side of the greenery as she climbed gingerly out the window and reached for the heavy limb.

"Daddy! Daaaddyyyy!"

❄ ❄ ❄

ZACH HEARD his daughter screaming for him, at the same time a ghostly voice shouted at him.

"Save Nat; Zach you must save Nat!"

He'd just gotten to his feet, and was on his way out of his office to check on Belle. It sounded like her voice came from the backyard, for god's sake. Why wasn't she safe and sound, watching TV in the playroom just off her bedroom where he'd left her?

"Belle!" He ran down the hall and flung open the door to an empty room. A quick look in her bedroom garnered the same results. "Belle!" he thundered. "Where are you?"

His heart in his throat, he tore downstairs and through the kitchen, yanking open the door to the yard, only to rock back as she flew into his arms.

"Quick, Daddy! Nat-alie. Her house is on fire. She's in the window!"

The adrenaline surge and subsequent relief had him grab the doorframe for support when he realized nothing had happened to his daughter. He clutched her to his chest, then propped her on his hip and jogged down the stairs toward the gate. He had a bad feeling his little girl hadn't stuck to his rules.

He popped open the gate at the side of the house, his heart about stopping when he saw smoke billowing from the back of Nat's home. Noooo! He couldn't lose her right after he'd realized how much she meant to him!

"You gots to hurry, Daddy! Come on. She's in the window and I don't think she can get out!"

He ran down the steps and jogged between the houses to the front yard. The smoke was thickening, and his heart raced, wondering how much of the flames had engulfed the old place. It must be tinderbox dry. He couldn't leave Belle out front, but didn't want to take her near the fire.

"No, Daddy. You hafta go in the back. That's where it's burning and where the lady is!"

Zach groaned as he realized his daughter had gone over to Nat's house against his orders. He was going to have a heart-to-heart with his little girl about following rules after this.

He flicked the catch on the gate to Natalie's backyard and ran in, lecturing as they went. "You stay at the very back of the yard, do you hear me? Don't. Move."

"I won't, Daddy, I pwomise. Just hurry! Look up, she's in the window!"

He ran to the fence at the back of the yard and set Belle down before turning and racing back to the house, horrified to see flames engulfing the entire porch and corner of the kitchen. The sirens he heard screaming in the distance better be headed here. He looked up at the window Belle had pointed to, only to find it empty. "Natalie!" he yelled.

"Here! I'm here, Zach!"

Coughing punctuated her cry as smoke changed direction and billowed around the old tree he saw her perched in. His heart skipped a beat to see her clutching the trunk of the big oak, stuck on a wide limb just six and a half feet from the ground, and about the same distance from the house, too far up to jump without hurting herself. He spied a wicked scar running the length of her shin and figured that was the reason she was having trouble getting out of the tree. She was low enough, though, that he'd be able to reach her hips and lift her down.

"Hold tight. I've got you!"

His eyes and lungs burned as he raced through the smoke and skidded to a stop under where she sat, relieved when the wind changed direction and whipped it back toward the house. He wrapped his hands around her hips, trying for careful when all he wanted to do was snatch her down and run like hell.

Their eyes met as she clutched the silky robe closed across her breasts with one hand, panic and pain washing across her pretty face.

"Hang on tight and bring your other leg to this side."

She followed his directions carefully, wobbling a little on the branch. He tightened his hold on her hips and was grateful she trusted him enough to grab his forearm with her free hand and lean down, depending on him to carry her to safety.

He lifted her from the tree branch and lowered her to the ground, wrapping an arm around her waist as she again clutched her robe closed. Relief washed through him when the wail of a siren and screech of brakes cut off abruptly in front of the house.

Her leg crumpled at her first step and he swept her into his arms, her gasp drowned out by the shouts of the firefighters. He jogged back to where his daughter was standing with her head down, tears dribbling down her cheeks. He lowered to sit on the cold ground, settling Natalie on his lap, one arm wrapped tight around Nat and the other around Belle, tugging her close.

His little girl burst into sobs and buried her face in his side, whether hiding from Natalie or just realizing now how much trouble she was going to be in for leaving the house.

"Hey, pumpkin. Everything's going to be fine."

"Okay, dad-daddy."

That look on his munchkin's face didn't bode well. It was the same guilty look she got when she broke something or disobeyed. He'd get to the bottom of that later. He'd noticed Nat's grimace when he'd sat down and asked, "Where are you hurt besides your leg?"

"I twisted my leg when I got out of the tub and fell, then hurt my head when I smacked it on the tree trunk climbing out the window. Other than that, I'm okay."

He looked at the abraded lump on her temple and cursed silently. Her teeth started chattering, and he wished he had a thick blanket to wrap her in to counter the shock of escaping her burning home, and the December chill of coastal weather.

❄ ❄ ❄

NATALIE FELT her nipples bead from the chill breeze and wished she had on her plush, warm robe instead of this barely there silky number. She wiggled to get comfortable in his lap and surprise lit her up inside to realize that, although her house was in flames, attraction for this big man had tingles zipping through her nerves.

Oh, she knew the attraction had been building over the past several weeks—if she was honest with herself—the seed had first taken root back when they'd met a couple of years ago. Wasn't that why she'd stopped inviting him over for meals? *What on earth was the matter with her?*

Her beloved grandma's house was burning in front of her eyes, her leg hurt like heck, her forehead throbbed from smacking it on the tree trunk, and she was half-naked on Zach's lap. *What the heck was she doing?* Thinking carnal thoughts about the darned man.

She'd felt nothing for *years*, since well before she'd lost Matty—when her ex-husband had first started his campaign of terror and abuse—not happiness, not desire, not much of anything at all. *Why now? With this man?* She just couldn't seem to ignore how muscular and much too sexy for her own good he was. How gentle, compassionate, and caring. She'd noticed it back when Calum had been in the hospital, but had been a basket-case then and not in any frame of mind to do anything about it.

Apparently, now that she was back in Beacon Bay and in close proximity to the darned man, her heart was finally thawing. She wasn't sure she approved. Wasn't it better to just let it stay frozen? Then there'd be no chance of being disappointed or having it broken again.

With her head tucked under his chin and sitting sideways on those muscled quads, she got an eyeful of his to-die-for body. A black tee shirt hugged the corded strength of his broad chest and shoulders. His biceps bulged like melons, especially with her added weight. His thighs were like thick tree limbs, rock hard and ripped.

Her eyes slid closed, and she reminded herself there were more important things to think about than what his body did to her libido. Like were her keepsakes—her only mementoes and reminders of Matty and her grandma—turning into a pile of ash along with the house she grew up in?

It was too much to take in, and no doubt she was using her attraction to the darned man to escape the fear and loss happening to her home and belongings.

She tucked her head deeper into the warmth of his neck, his male-musk and strength a double-edged sword. Her pounding heart tripped to a different beat as she breathed him in, its cadence finally slowing from fear to the steady beat of his own heart.

His now escalating heartbeat, she realized, ratcheting even faster when she wiggled again to get even closer to the delicious heat of his body. He apparently wasn't unaffected by her in his lap after all, unless the fear of his daughter being out of the house, and saving her from the fire, had him ramped up. Adrenaline overload. That was probably it. Happened to men on the battlefield all the time.

She told herself sternly there was no way she was going to act on this unwanted attraction, even if he reciprocated. Not only was she still trying to get her head on straight from her surgeries and losing her grandma, and still depressed by the loss of her little guy, she was busy with her business—and not interested in the opposite sex.

Besides, she couldn't be around his little girl for any length of time. It was just too painful. It seemed like only yesterday she'd lost Matty and sadness still consumed her. She carefully blanked her brain and concentrated on letting the heat from his body chase away the chill.

"Daddy? Is the lady going to be okay?" she heard Belle whisper.

"Yes, pumpkin. She's going to be fine."

"But her house, Daddy."

Zach motioned the paramedics over as they ran through the gate into the backyard. "Hey, over here!"

The two-woman team jogged across the yard and squatted, one laying out their equipment while the other got busy with Natalie.

"Let's look at your eyes and that bump on your head," she murmured. As she shone a penlight in each eye and checked Natalie's pupils, she asked, "How long did you breathe smoke?"

"Not long. The wind only blew in my direction for a few seconds before reversing again, right before Zach pulled me out of the tree."

"Good, that's good. Eyes look fine," the med tech murmured, apparently satisfied smoke inhalation would not be an immediate problem. "Let's get this nasal cannula on you and some oxygen going just in case until the doc can check you out at the hospital."

"Oh, I don't need to go to the hospital. I'm good," Natalie countered through chattering teeth.

The paramedic was having none of that and pinned her with a glare as she tucked the tubing behind her ears and notched it in her nose. "Be smart. If not for yourself, then for your husband and daughter. Smoke inhalation is nothing to mess with, nor is a head injury."

Natalie stiffened at the paramedic's words. There was a small corner of her heart that wondered what it would be like to be Zach's wife and Belle's mama.

"I know, you're right, I just hate hospitals. I've spent way too much time there."

She glanced up when Zach dipped his head down and realized she hadn't masked the distress or emotional pain well enough. She let her eyes drift shut—too upset, too exhausted and in too darned much pain—to decipher the emotions she'd seen swirl in his.

He leaned over until his lips brushed her ear. "A trip to the emergency room is a good idea, Nat."

"I don't need to go, honestly." She kept her eyes closed. No way did she want to see the compassion in his eyes or his pretty little girl any longer than necessary. And no way did she want to step foot in a hospital again. The smells and bright lights brought back memories best left buried.

"Don't be stubborn," he growled. "Smoke inhalation and concussions aren't something to ignore. You need to have a doctor sign off."

Her eyes opened and met his. "I appreciate your help, really, but I'm not going to the hospital. The paramedics can finish checking me out here."

She attempted to get off his lap when the paramedic stood and he tugged her right back down, garnering a huff from her at his highhandedness. His big, callused hand on her cheek as he tugged her around to look at him had her stilling.

"Do I need to call Cal?"

Well, darn him for knowing just what to say to get her to agree with him, and the paramedic.

"Fine, I'll go, but you don't need to go with me. And do *not* call Calum."

Chapter Eight

NAT WAS STILL arguing with him when Zach pulled into his driveway four hours later. The threat of calling Calum had convinced her to let them take her in the ambulance to the hospital, and he'd followed in his truck with a subdued Belle riding along. He'd finally reached her cousin at a physical therapy symposium downtown, and he'd met Zach in the hospital waiting room.

They'd treated Nat for mild smoke inhalation, and had proclaimed she had a mild concussion from whacking her forehead on the tree, as well as having re-injured her leg. She'd be off it for a few days, then could ease into walking again and continue PT. The emergency room had been blessedly quiet, and they'd had her in and out in just under a couple of hours. He'd actually gone weak-kneed with relief when the doc had proclaimed her none the worse for having breathed in the toxic smoke.

"You can just drop me off at Calum's," Natalie groused. "There's no reason for me to stay with you."

"I'm not dropping you off at Calum's. You'd never get any sleep on his short couch. Did you not listen to the doc when he said to stay off that leg, and you should have someone monitor you for a few days from that knock on your hard head? You can't even walk by yourself."

When she opened her mouth, no doubt to argue some more, he placed a finger across her lips. "Cal has a full schedule, and I told you I'm on vacation and available until after Christmas—heck, for as long as you need me—and have an extra room, too, with a big comfy bed. Staying with me makes more sense, now and while they repair your house. The doctor and Calum vetoed you staying at his place or in a hotel, and both encouraged you to stay here. Am I such an ogre you can't stand the thought of being in the same house as me? Quit being so stubborn and let me help you. It's not like I'm really a stranger, anyway. I've been friends with Cal for over ten years, and I thought you and I were becoming friends over the past few weeks, if not the week we spent years ago."

"Fine! You're as hard-headed as he is," she snapped, then continued in a subdued voice. " And I don't think you're an ogre at all. We are—friends."

Her voice so low at the end, he'd almost missed her comment about being friends, and wondered at the hesitation before she said 'friends'. Did she think of him as more than a friend?

As he climbed from the vehicle, he shook his head. He needed to figure a way to help her be comfortable in his home—without coming on too strong.

Although convinced she had feelings for him that surpassed friendship, he would ensure he did nothing to make her uncomfortable while she recuperated and had nowhere else to go. He'd learned iron control during MARSOC training and on the battlefield—he'd just have to use that control and make sure he didn't cross a line with her. Unless, of course, she gave any sign she wanted him to. Then all bets were off.

"Wait here while I get Belle settled in bed and I'll come back out to help you into the house."

"I can make it that short distance."

"Damn, woman, you're as stubborn as your cousin. Please, just wait here for me. Your leg is unstable, and it's buckled every time you've put that foot down. You keep it up and you'll have a permanent injury. Besides, the doc said to stay off it. I will not risk another bonk on your head if you fall, or have you mess up your leg even worse than it is. Can't you put aside your stubbornness for five minutes while I get Belle settled?"

He ignored her grumbling and lifted his sleeping munchkin from the backseat. His mouth quirked as she drooled on his shoulder, but a backward glance wiped the smile right off his face.

The glimmer of pain in Natalie's eyes as she watched his daughter reminded him of the pain when he'd almost lost Belle, the pain she must feel at not having her son tragically worse, because her pain was permanent. To lose a child would tear the heart right from a mother's chest, and his arms tightened around his daughter at the thought.

"Daddy, too tight." Her sleepy voice brought him out of his nightmarish memories.

"Sorry, pumpkin. Let's get you to bed." He dropped a kiss on her silky hair, thankful again for the skills he'd learned in the military. For a long time afterwards, he never wanted to let her out of his sight—had to relearn how to share her with his sister.

He made it upstairs and tucked Belle in bed without changing her clothes. If she woke fully while getting PJs on, she'd be underfoot while he got Nat settled, and he knew the poor woman was still on edge from the trauma of almost losing her home and her visit to the hospital.

As he turned to leave, Belle mumbled, "Want Mr. King, Daddy." He reversed his steps and snuggled her furry friend under the covers. She wrapped her little arm around the king's neck and was fast asleep.

He all but ran down the stairs, not trusting Natalie to stay in the truck. He'd never met a more contrary woman or man. Jesus, she could give lessons in stubbornness.

When he jogged back outside and to the truck, he saw she'd dropped her head back against the seat and closed her eyes, probably exhausted beyond measure.

"Hey, you okay?"

Her eyes flew open. "Oh! You know, I'd really be fine at Calum's. I don't want to trouble you."

He slanted her a look and ignored her repeated attempt to have him drop her at Cal's. "Come on. Let's get you inside and to bed."

Opening the door, he scooped her up in his arms, reveling in the feel of her curvy body held snug against his chest. His heart skipped a beat, then raced when she tucked her face into the curve of his neck, sound asleep before they made it through the front door and into the living room.

Relief filled Zach when he felt Nat go from stiff to supple in a heartbeat. He blew out a frustrated breath at her continued arguments for staying anywhere but his house. He wondered how much of that was from wanting to keep her distance from Belle, and how much was because she was fighting her attraction to him?

He valiantly tried to ignore the way his body reacted to having her in his arms. The hospital had given her scrubs to wear, the thin layer of cotton between her silky skin and his bare hands and forearms driving him crazy. He was a Marine, for God's sake. He'd trained to withstand pain. To keep going when he felt ready to drop dead. To ignore distractions. To keep his eye on the target.

His body, mind—and possibly his heart—had all decided *she* was the target, though. He needed to pay attention, dammit, to what was important. Helping her get back on her feet—*and* convincing her to give them a chance.

He topped the stairs and strode into the spare bedroom to the bed. The sheet already pulled back, he laid her gently in the middle of the mattress. As he pulled the covers over her long legs, he couldn't resist dropping a kiss on her forehead.

He grinned a little when he realized he'd finally gotten the kiss he'd been craving, even if it wasn't on her enticingly full lips.

Chapter Nine

NAT STIFFENED AS she came awake suddenly, aware someone was in the room with her. She jerked in alarm, stars swirling in front of her eyes when pain exploded in her head. The chocolate-brown eyes staring at her from a little elfin face, and the unrelenting pain in her head confused her.

Where was she?

She closed her eyes wearily, her head sinking back into the soft pillow as yesterday's events bombarded her mind. Escape from her burning home and earning a concussion, re-injuring her leg, and smoke inhalation to boot. And that she'd caved and was in Zach's house. She must have zonked out right after he'd took her into his muscular arms when they got back from the hospital.

It doubly confused her when Belle whispered, "I'm sorry." What the heck was that about? She rolled to her side and pushed up to sit against the headboard, peering down at the little girl, the pain meds and exhaustion making her loopy. *What am I going to do when being anywhere near a child just about breaks my heart?*

Make the best of it was pretty much her only choice. Her leg was sore, her forehead throbbed, and her bladder was about to burst. As much as she hated to admit it, she needed help to get to the bathroom.

At the sound of Zach striding down the hallway, she sighed, absurdly tempted to pull a pillow over her head. Deciding to be an adult about this, she left the pillow where it was and watched warily as he rounded the doorway and stopped, one hand on a lean hip, a bundle of clothing clutched in the other.

A part of her, that part that had been growing closer to him over the past few weeks, the part that admired him and loved—nope, *liked* pretty much everything about him—wanted nothing more than to be close to him. To give in and let him care for her while she recuperated.

It had been years—since she was young and living with her grandma—that anyone had taken care of her and made her feel she was worth something. That she was important. Zach made her feel that way, and along with these new feelings, her heart felt resurrected—like the dead parts were healing, the damage reversing—and she reveled in the new feelings practically bursting to get out.

It terrified her to embrace these new feelings, though. Giving in could hurt all three of them. Zach and Belle could get attached, and then realize her heart was damaged beyond repair. Not worth the effort. Unable to love anyone ever again.

If she opened her heart to Zach, and also opened it to Belle, then ran like a scared rabbit, little Belle and her daddy would be sad. She would have brought disharmony into their close-knit, amazing little family. No way did she want to do that.

Nope, it would be better, smarter, if she just recuperated, kept them both at arm's length, then burrowed into her grandma's house again—if it wasn't a pile of ash inside. She couldn't bring herself to look, or to ask.

❄ ❄ ❄

ZACH STRODE into the room, wondering why Belle was there and sorry to see Natalie squinting in pain, a lost, distant look in her eyes. He set his sister's clothes on the foot of the bed and picked Belle up, giving her a smacking kiss on the cheek before setting her back on her feet with a gentle push toward the door.

"Hot chocolate is on the table, sweetpea. I'll be right down."

"Okay, Daddy." Belle looked shyly at Natalie before darting toward the door and into the hall, calling back to him. "You should kiss her booboo. It always makes me feel better."

Zach's eyes snapped to Natalie's. His daughter's innocent words held a completely different meaning for him. He'd like to kiss more than her booboo. His libido wanted him to kiss every inch of that silky skin.

He bet he'd be able to make her forget all her aches and pains, and cause a few *good* aches in some secret places. His cock started its salute when he saw her eyes darken with awareness—of him as a man. A man who wanted her naked and under him. He'd seen that look off and on many times in the past few weeks, when he'd caught her gaze on him before she could bank her thoughts behind a casual expression.

He willed his unruly little head to behave itself, not wanting to make her uncomfortable. "You probably need to use the bathroom about now."

He saw no way around it. He had to lay his hands on all that smooth, sweet flesh to get her from point A to point B. The doctor had concerns about her concussion, and had told her to stay off that unstable leg. No way was he letting her out of bed without his help.

He'd sure better get used to ignoring and tamping down this attraction bombarding him at every turn, or he'd be walking around with a permanent hard-on. His cock would be tattooed from head to base by his zipper.

Just the memory of them in her backyard, her lush bottom on his thighs separated by nothing but a thin layer of silk, had him about bursting out of his jeans. All she had to do was drop her gaze to his crotch, and she'd get an eyeful. She'd discover he had absolutely no control whatsoever when he was near her.

Or maybe she'd think he was this way around any woman? Little did she know he hadn't had a spontaneous erection, except his morning wood, in five long years. Until her.

She pulled back the covers and slid her legs over the side, gracing him with his first unobstructed glimpse of her shapely legs. He bit back a wince at the long, pink scar marring her shin from knee to ankle. Man, that had to have hurt.

His t-shirt only hit her at mid-thigh and looked a hell of a lot better draped over her unbound breasts than it ever did on him. Those lightly muscled thighs and calves were going to be the death of him. How was he supposed to stay upright when all the blood went south and settled between his legs?

He tamped down his reaction and handed her the clothes he'd brought in. "These are some of my sister's clothes—yoga pants and a tank top. Pretty sure they'll fit okay."

When he scooped her into his arms, sweat beaded his forehead as the silky skin of those luscious legs brushed against the palm of his hand and forearm. When his fingers grazed the swell of her breast, he thought he'd died and gone to heaven. He needed to get his shit together and tamp down this damned attraction.

He set her next to the sink and couldn't stop from giving her hand a squeeze before stepping back. "I'll wait in the bedroom. There's a new toothbrush in the cabinet. I'll bring you down for breakfast when you're done."

He stifled a grin at her sigh. As reluctant as he knew her to be, she seemed finally resigned to his help, which was a darned good thing. Little did she know he could win medals in stubbornness.

He heard a flush and the faucet run briefly, and waited impatiently until the knob rattled and a stifled curse cut the silence. In two steps he was at the door, pulling it open only to have his arms full of curvy, warm woman.

"Umf!" Her eyes snapped to his as soft breasts collided with his pecs.

If he thought having her in his arms earlier was hard to handle, having her lithe body plastered against his from breast to thigh was pure torture. There was no way she could miss the hard ridge of his arousal pulsing against her stomach. A groan escaped before he could call it back.

Her arms tightened seductively around his waist and she actually nuzzled his shoulder before she pushed back, wiggling to get free. She no doubt realized giving him mixed signals would get her more than she'd bargained for.

"Hold on, Nat, you'll hurt yourself. Dammit, Natalie." He once again scooped her into his arms, halting her desperate struggle. His cock mourned the loss of all that sweet flesh pressed against it.

Her beaded nipples, clearly outlined under the t-shirt, accelerated pulse, and the bright flush washing across her pretty cheekbones told him better than words she felt the same electricity he did when they touched.

He hoped they would both be able to settle into being comfortable with each other, despite their mutual attraction, and her discomfort around Belle. She was under so much stress, both old and new, and he wanted nothing more than to help her through this. His body and libido would just have to take a seat and let his heart lead.

The poor woman, with the recent loss of her grandma, and now possibly all her possessions inside her charred and waterlogged home, had to be about at the end of her rope.

And boy, did he understand loss. He'd also suffered loss of independence and mobility during his last tour of duty. His injury hadn't taken as long to heal as hers, but he understood the soul-sucking frustration of not being fully mobile and independent. Of not being able to take care of yourself.

He understood loss of a child to some degree, too, having lost Belle years ago, even if only for a few hours. And then losing his mother right after he'd recovered his daughter.

Yeah, he understood, all right. And he planned to be the one to help her through this loss, if only as a friend—although he wanted much, much more.

Chapter Ten

ZACH PRESSED THE button to end the call and turned to Natalie. They'd finished breakfast in tense silence and it was past time to get her to therapy. "Cal's ready for you."

She raised her eyes from her steaming cup of coffee. "I think I'll skip today."

"He said he just wants to evaluate, to see if he needs to change or reduce your therapy since you re-injured your leg. Honestly, I think he just needs to see you with his own eyes to make sure you're okay."

"I'm not up to him badgering me, Zach."

"Cal won't badger you today. I know he can and will, when necessary, to get us to do therapy, but that's not the vibe I got from him over the phone. Besides, you know he'll be here to get you himself if I don't deliver you to his door. You don't want to pull him away from his other patients just because you're being stubborn, do you? I know you've got to be tired. I'll bring you right back afterwards, and if it gets to be too much when you're there, just call me and I'll spring you."

If he had to play the guilt card, so be it. He was afraid if she hid away, she'd start sliding back into that deep depression she'd been mired in weeks ago when she first arrived. Her demeanor and mood had much improved over the days and weeks they'd been sharing meals and spending time together. No way did he want to see her slide back into that dark place.

"Fine," she sighed. "I'm ready to go now. I can shower and change clothes afterwards."

"I'm hoping you'll feel better after, but I meant what I said. Call me if it's too much for you, and I'll pick you up right away."

Her nod of acquiescence had him grabbing his keys and wallet before turning to his daughter.

"Belle honey, grab Mr. King and let's go. Natalie needs to go see Uncle Calum."

Zach eyed Natalie as her hooded eyes tracked Belle when she jumped from her chair and skipped out of the kitchen. He knew being around his little girl was torturous for her, but what could he do? No way would he banish Belle to her room for the duration of Nat's stay.

His heart tightened when she turned turbulent moss-green and gold flecked eyes his way. They seemed to be begging him for something, but for the life of him, he couldn't figure out what she needed. Or wanted.

He brushed a finger down her smooth cheek, mesmerized by what looked like affection flashing through her eyes.

"I'm gonna carry you to the truck."

At her nod, he slid an arm under her thighs and one behind her back, scooping her against his chest. Felt like it was right where she belonged. When she tucked her face under his chin, he beat back that insistent voice in his heart and soul proclaiming, "Mine!"

"Daddddy!"

Zach breathed a sigh of relief when Belle skidded back into the room and broke the intimate moment.

"Okay, let's go or you'll be late. You don't want Calum to scold you." His teasing grin softened his words as they followed his little angel skipping down the hall.

He strode to the truck and set Natalie on her good foot to open the passenger door, then helped her onto the seat. After settling Belle in the back, he circled the hood and opened the driver's door.

The drive to Cal's took less than five minutes. Belle had been unusually quiet on the ride over and once he dropped Natalie off, he was going to find out why she'd been subdued since the fire. He was getting a bad feeling about the cause of it.

He unbuckled Belle, lifted her out of the truck and set her on her feet, then scooped his reluctant passenger into his arms again. "Don't worry, you'll be back on your feet in no time and won't have to put up with me carrying you around."

She mumbled something, and his eyes jerked to hers, to see her avert her gaze. He could have sworn she'd said, "I don't mind." No, he had to be mistaken. He knew she felt this attraction they shared, maybe as much as he did, but he didn't think she'd encourage him. Or that she was actually ready to pursue the heat they generated whenever they were within five feet of each other. He was pretty sure he was miles ahead of her in wanting to pursue a relationship, and she was still struggling with the thought of opening herself up to one. Especially to a man with a kid.

He could be wrong, though. Lord knew he'd been wrong in the past. A man could hope, though.

"Belle, push the button to open the door, please."

Zach waited while the automatic door slowly opened, then followed Belle into the therapy room and stopped. Calum was working with a pretty young woman across the room. It didn't surprise him to see concern in his buddy's eyes as he helped the woman do leg lifts on a machine.

What *did* surprise him was the flicker of attraction that darkened Calum's eyes when her sweat-stained tank pulled up, exposing a four-pack and colorful hummingbird tattoo low on one side.

"Hey, buddy. Where does Natalie need to be?"

Even more interesting was the flash of guilt in Calum's eyes—at being caught ogling his patient? If Zach wasn't mistaken, Calum's hand on her shoulder seemed possessive. More like a caress. *Very Interesting*, he thought. He couldn't wait to get Calum alone to grill him.

"On that bench in the corner," Cal said with a nod, apparently unaware his long fingers still gripped the woman's shoulder, his thumb caressing the bare skin above her tank.

"I'll hook you up to the CPM machine to get your knee warmed up, Nat," Calum continued. "You said you've used the continuous passive motion machine before, right?"

Natalie gave a nod. "Yes, since a week after my last surgery. The doc in Portland said I could start on calf and thigh exercises this week, too, although with re-injuring it yesterday, I'm not sure that's still okay."

"We'll evaluate and see. You may need to just use the CPM for a few days to see how it goes. After the CPM, I'll get you started on light thigh strengthening with a band loop, just above your knees. No extra weight on that tibia yet, or your knee."

Zach hated the thought of leaving her, but knew she was in expert, caring hands with her cousin. He knew Calum wouldn't let her get away with doing anything that would damage her leg, and wouldn't let her leave without Zach being there to take her home. He glanced down at the tug on his hand.

"Daddy, are we going to get our tree now? You pwomised we could go this week. How many days did you say until Christmas?"

"Just a few, sweetpea, and yes, we'll get the tree today."

He bit back a smile at the scandalized look on Belle's face when she must have realized the holiday was only a few days away, and they still didn't have a tree. Christmas was her favorite holiday, next to Halloween, and he'd been super busy, putting off getting the tree till much later than usual.

He glanced at Natalie and his smile fell away at the shadows swirling in her eyes, knowing she ached for her son. And now missed her grandma. He imagined what the holiday would be like without Belle and would bet the bank Natalie hadn't celebrated a holiday, much less life itself, since she'd lost her little boy.

With a nod at Calum, he glanced back at Nat and looped his little finger with hers, giving it a squeeze. He could see the pulse in her neck jittering when he linked his pinky with hers, it somehow being almost more intimate than a kiss. It linked them together, brought a solidarity to their—what—their relationship? Did they have a relationship of some kind after weeks of spending time together? That look of affection that flashed in her eyes brought warmth to his soul and hope to his heart.

"I'll be back for you, sweetheart."

Zach could tell Natalie was biting back a comment, probably not wanting to hurt Belle's or his feelings, but he'd bet no way did she want anything to do with Christmas or a tree.

He glanced back at her cousin, still holding her finger with his. "We'll be back in about an hour. That enough time?"

"Sure." Calum nodded absently, still concentrating on the woman at his side. "Sounds good."

❄ ❄ ❄

"YO, BUDDY, Natalie ready to be picked up?" Zach held Belle in one arm, juggling a shopping bag with the same hand, while he held his phone to one ear with his other hand.

"She's bitching and doing her best to talk me into letting her stay at my house. Promise you won't cave if she starts in on you. I know it's a lot to ask, man, but I just can't see her staying on my couch for however many weeks it takes for her house to get fixed up. And I won't be able to monitor her and ensure she stays off that leg."

"No worries." He leaned down to set Belle on a bench outside their favorite model train store, This Little Engine Could. They'd picked up a new caboose for their Christmas train, and had been ready to grab something to eat when he realized it was time to pick up his reluctant roommate.

"Hey, confession time. I overheard you talking to her about Matty, through her open window the day she arrived a few weeks ago. When I was taking out the trash. You and I had talked about it before, but I didn't realize she blamed herself, and didn't know he'd been the same age as Belle."

Calum's pained sigh came through clearly. "Yeah, I should have told you already, what with Belle being the same age Matty was when he died."

"I was afraid you were going to say something like that."

"Hang on a minute, I'm gonna step into my office, then you need to get over here and take her off my hands. PT was pretty painful, and she's on a short fuse. I know Belle will help diffuse it, though."

"You got it. Just give me the Cliff's Notes version for now."

"Okay, bullet points for now. I mentioned before she'd been married to a real son–of–a-bitch. Flipped a switch and started being physically abusive right after she had Matty. She kicked him out and filed for divorce immediately, got a restraining order, for all the good that did. Fast forward four years, he's out of prison early for good behavior. What a crock of bull. He shows up out of the blue, kidnaps her and Matty at gunpoint. Crashes the car, killing himself, and that sweet little boy."

Zach hated putting his friend through the retelling, but if he was going to be caring for Natalie, if he had any hope at all of a relationship with her, he didn't want to step on any emotional landmines and blow either of them up. He waited silently while his buddy pulled it together.

Cal cleared his throat, his voice hoarse when he continued. "Nat was in critical condition for two months. Almost lost her leg. Has been re-injuring it off and on since then. I think subconsciously she's doing it on purpose. Now that she's here, I'm going to make sure she gets back on her feet. Physically and emotionally."

Zach turned his head a little and lowered his voice so Belle wouldn't hear. "Thanks man. I want to lay my cards out with you. I don't think you buy into that 'not with my sister or cousin, you're not' bullshit. You may not have noticed," he paused, then continued, "but I'd love nothing more than for Nat to decide she wants to be with me. For the long haul. I'm just not sure how to help her be comfortable with Belle. Learn to love her, and me."

"You've got that right, buddy—I don't buy into that BS. I was actually hoping you two would click and get together. That's the reason I didn't tell you she was moving here. So you could both meet again without prior warning, or preconceived notions about how the other person was going to act, or be able to shore up any emotional walls. I honestly wasn't sure about you, what with Jo Ann's antics with drugs and then her kidnapping Belle. I'm glad to see you come around. Now, if you can just be patient with Nat, I think she will too. I've seen the way she looks at you, Zach. Longing, lots of affection. I'm ignoring any lustworthy looks you two are tossing back and forth, though."

Zach chuckled and shook his head. "You're a devious one, my man, and always have been. Shoulda known you had something up your sleeve, with never being able to pick her up for PT or drive her home."

"Yeah, yeah. Get down here and take her off my hands, man. She's ready to head out by herself if she has to crawl. And treat her right, or I'll have your hide."

"Wouldn't have it any other way. Be there soon."

He pocketed his phone and turned to his munchkin. "Belle, let's go get Natalie. Uncle Cal says she doesn't feel well, so we'll just let her rest on the way home. Let's not ask her questions, okay?"

"But Daddy! What about the tree we picked out?"

"I'm having it delivered, honey. Natalie's in too much pain to go with us, and I don't want to leave her home by herself. They'll deliver it this afternoon. Don't pay any attention if she's a little grumpy, okay?"

"Um, okay. She probably won't talk to me anyway, Daddy. I think she doesn't like me, cause she looks at me funny, like she's mad at me."

"Oh, sweetpea, she's not mad. She's sad. She had a little boy years ago, but he died, so I think she doesn't know how to act around kids anymore." Zach had waffled about whether to tell his daughter about Matty, but decided Belle needed to know any attitude from Nat wasn't her fault.

"That's so sad, Daddy. I bet she misses him bad." Belle slipped her thumb in her mouth, something she hadn't done in years. She slanted him a glance that slid away to stare at her shoes and mumbled around her thumb, "Is she mad about the fire, Daddy? Sometimes fires are accidents, right?"

Alarms started going off in Zach's head at her questions. He couldn't shake the feeling Belle had something to do with the fire.

Zach squatted down in front of his daughter and gently pulled her thumb from her mouth. "Look at me, sweetpea. You know I love you more than anything ever, right? And that nothing will ever change that?"

She turned dark-chocolate eyes swimming in tears to him. "Yes, Daddy."

"You know we're always honest with each other, right? Belle, did you have something to do with how the fire started at Natalie's house? No one's going to be mad at you."

His heart about broke to see her little lip quivering as she whispered, "I just wanted to turn the lights on, Daddy. I thought she should have lights, too, and maybe she wouldn't be mean anymore, cause lights are happy. So I plugged them in."

Zach tugged Belle into his arms and wondered how he was going to tell Natalie his daughter had set her house on fire.

Chapter Eleven

WHEN ZACH WALKED through Cal's clinic door and glimpsed Nat's stressed expression, he wondered if he could get away with killing his friend. It was a good thing his other patient had left. He'd hate to have a witness to Cal's murder. He could just make out what they were saying and stayed quiet so he could eavesdrop.

"If you won't let me stay here, then just call me a cab, Calum. For God's sake, how do you think I survived all this time without someone taking care of me? I'll meet Zach at his house."

She must have caught sight of him, because she stopped trying to talk Cal into letting her stay. Her eyes widened when Zach stalked across the room, looking no doubt like a storm-trooper ready to give Calum what-for.

"Not his fault, Zach," she said softly as he reached her side, then surprised him by taking his hand in hers, and linking their fingers together. "We were just snarking at each other."

The soft plea in her voice worked like magic, and he felt his anger deflate. She didn't need him to come to her rescue, as much as that protective part of him wanted to. She needed his support, and to make her life easier while she recuperated. At *his* home, dammit.

Zach still wanted nothing more than to flatten his friend. Tough love was one thing, but Cal needed to back off. He had no clue what they'd been arguing about, but maybe he and Cal just needed to let Natalie set her own pace. Maybe tough love wasn't what she needed.

Although, his buddy had needed a little tough love himself when they'd come back from that shithole he'd lost part of his leg in. But still. His good buddy needed to learn to dish out his advice in small doses, not ram it down her throat.

Zach's injury had been nothing like Cal's. His friend left a piece of himself back there. Literally. It took a year of badgering and getting in his face to get him back on his remaining foot and out of the bottle. But it was worth every minute, and every black eye, when he didn't duck fast enough and Cal's fist made a solid connection.

Choosing to ignore rather than smack him, Zach kept possession of Natalie's hand and said lightly, "Let's blow this pop stand, honey. Belle picked out a large pepperoni and extra cheese from Pie Town across the street. Just need to pop it in the oven. Ready to head home?"

He could feel Belle vibrating with the need to join the conversation and hoped she remembered what he'd said. He was sure his little girl was on pins and needles as to how Natalie would react to hearing she'd caused the fire, but apparently the idea of pizza and a Christmas tree trumped her worry. At least for now. He didn't think Natalie could take a conversation with Belle about Christmas trees and decorating on the short ride home, though.

He knew it was too good to be true when Belle took Natalie's other hand with her sticky little fingers and tugged. Belle leaned in close, as if to keep him from hearing her. He tensed, unsure what she'd say. Spontaneous confession or Christmas talk?

"I'm not supposed to talk much cause your leg hurts and you're sad, but maybe if you help us decorate the tree, you'll feel better."

Zach groaned and wrapped his hand gently around Belle's little arm, meaning to pull her away. He stopped, mesmerized by the flash of affection he saw in Natalie's glistening eyes when she looked down at his daughter.

"Belle, honey," Zach murmured.

"Shhh." Natalie glanced at him, then back down at his daughter.

"That's very sweet of you, Belle. Why don't we wait to see how I feel when we get to your house, okay?"

Zach appreciated Natalie being upfront with Belle, and in a way that didn't hurt her feelings. She didn't lie or skate around the subject, either.

"Thank you," he whispered as he leaned in and swept Natalie into his arms, nodding to Cal as he turned.

"How about helping me get Belle settled in her seat, bro."

"You got it. I expect to see you back tomorrow, Nat. I want ice on that knee tonight, twenty on, forty off, times four. Got it?"

Zach's mouth quirked when he caught Natalie rolling her eyes at her cousin. His grin turned strained when she wiggled to get comfortable in his arms and his fingers brushed the underside of her plump breast. Her gaze snapped to his as they both tensed.

He willed his little head to behave as it bumped his zipper. Wanting attention, again. Like her slim hands or lush mouth wrapped around it. He made quick work of getting her settled in his truck, thankful his munchkin and Cal were chaperoning, so he didn't give into the urge to drop a kiss on her plump lips.

As he pulled away from the curb, he realized it would be a lesson in iron control to wait and hope Natalie's feelings came around to match his. He wouldn't curb all his affection, though. The woman was blatantly starved for touch, for caring—for love—soaking it up like a new sponge on the beach, being washed over by the ocean tide.

Almost home, he glanced across the truck to see Natalie staring out the passenger window. Apparently lost in thought for the short ride home, no doubt used to being by herself—to protecting her heart at all costs—as he'd found out from Cal tattling on her.

And apparently much too used to being mired in depression and pain—both physical and emotional. If only she'd let him, he could replace love and affection with most of the depression, maybe help her memories become less painful, encourage her to share the good times she had with her little guy—help her lesson the pain all around.

"Hey." Zach closed a hand over her clenched fist. "You okay?" He'd called her name twice, but she'd been too deep in thought to respond. She glanced his way and nodded, but stayed mute with a stubborn tilt to her head.

He pulled into his drive and reversed their routine, getting everyone into the house and settling Natalie on a kitchen chair. A flick of his wrist had the oven preheating. He squatted on his heels and dropped a kiss on Belle's forehead.

"Get settled in the living room with a book, pumpkin. Be good and stay there till I come get you for dinner, okay?"

Belle peeked sideways at Natalie and shot him a look he now knew was full of guilt. He'd have to clue Natalie in, and soon, so his little girl would quit creeping around the house, waiting for the hammer to drop.

God, he didn't relish *that* conversation. *How will Natalie react?* As tense as she was, and clearly in pain from PT, now was not the time to spill the beans about the fire.

At Belle's hesitation, he stood and took her hand, walking her to the living room. "Come on, pumpkin. I'm going to get the pizza in the oven, and they'll deliver the tree soon."

He settled his little girl with her favorite *Lowly Worm* book and hurried back to the kitchen. The more he learned about Natalie, the more he understood her independent streak. She'd turned herself into a loner after having been a wife and mother, not to mention loving grandchild to her doting grandma, and more sister to Calum than cousin.

Now that she only had Cal left, he wondered if the transformation was complete and irreversible? The glimpse of her softening toward Belle—and the flashes of longing and affection for him that slipped through her barricade—lent him hope he, and Belle, would be able to breach the barricade around her heart. That, and the flare of desire in her eyes whenever he held her supple body in his arms.

Even if they didn't act on their mutual attraction, he held hope she would open her heart to someone, someday. He squelched the flare of jealously at the thought that someone would be another man, and not him. She didn't need that vibe from him.

Her soft voice jerked him from his brooding. "If you can help me to my room, you and Belle can have dinner together and do the tree without a third wheel."

"How about staying down here to eat and hanging with us while we decorate? You can give your opinions on where to hang the decorations. Can't have a lopsided tree."

He ignored her irritated look and clenched teeth, deciding to cut her off at the pass. "I know I'm not the boss of you, but I'm also not going to let you spend the entire time you're here, tucked away in your room. How is that healthy for you? At least stay until you've eaten—we'll get ice on that knee—and they deliver the tree. Then, if you're determined to be alone, I'll carry you to your room. Let me at least feed you. Please, Nat?"

He grabbed a flexible ice pack from the fridge, one that was in a sleeve that would wrap around her leg, and had Velcro to secure it, and handed it to her. He could tell his autocratic ways were annoying her, but no way was he going to let her get into the habit of hiding out upstairs. It was just too darned bad if she felt he was bossing her around. He'd never learned to quell his natural leadership and wasn't about to start now. She'd just have to suck it up and deal with him. At least tacking on the *please* at the end seemed to soften her expression and demeanor.

He'd been bossy before being MARSOC, had learned ninja-bossing skills as a Marine, and would probably be bossing the undertaker around from the afterlife.

At the ding of the oven, he grabbed the pizza and slid it onto the middle rack, set the timer for the pie, and one for the ice on her knee, then stepped to her side and lay a hand on her shoulder. "You need the loo before we eat?"

She shivered at his touch. "No, Calum helped me at his place." Stubbornness replaced the sensual fire that flashed in her eyes. "You know, I'm not going to mooch off you while I'm here. You need to at least let me contribute to the food budget, since I can't help around the house."

He rolled with her mercurial moods and topic switch, answering easily, "Sure, no problem. We'll get that figured out tomorrow." He understood her need to feel independent and knew paying her way would help curb her feelings of helplessness. He wasn't going to be a controlling asshole.

He could see her gearing up for another comment, thankfully saved from further discussion when Belle poked her head into the room.

"Daddy, when is the tree getting here? Is the pizza ready? I'm hungry."

"It should be here before we're done eating. Why don't you finish your book? I'll get Natalie something to drink and bring in the decorations. You can lay them out for us while the pizza's cooking."

Belle sidled up next to him and pulled on his hand so she could whisper in his ear. "Did you tell her, Daddy?"

Zach shook his head and glanced sideways to see Natalie narrow her eyes at him, apparently not having lost the keen hearing or intuition of a mother.

Chapter Twelve

BELLE'S EYES FLICKERED to Natalie, then spun back toward the hallway at the peal of the doorbell and froze, stock still. She jerked her head to look at Zach with wide, terrified eyes.

"It's okay, sweetie. Just the tree delivery," he said calmly. "Why don't you stay with Natalie while I pay and bring it into the living room?"

He tensed when Belle turned and launched herself at Nat, burying her sweet face in soft breasts and shivering like a leaf.

"Why, what….?" Natalie stammered.

He shook his head and mouthed *later.* As he strode from the room, he cursed his ex-girlfriend to the devil where she belonged.

After tipping the delivery girl and lugging the tree into the living room, he hurried back to the kitchen to find Natalie rocking Belle while singing about a teddy bear.

He could tell she was having trouble balancing a shivering Belle on her lap while keeping weight off her sore leg.

An uncharacteristic burning in his eyes caught him by surprise to see her cuddling his little girl. Belle raised glassy eyes to his as he pulled a chair next to them and lay a hand on her trembling shoulder.

"Daddy, I don't like the doorbell."

"I know, sweetie. It hasn't bothered you in a long time, though. Why tonight?"

"Because I like having Nat-alie here with us and I don't want to go away again, Daddy."

He met Natalie's eyes over his daughter's ebony hair. "Belle, honey. There's no way in the world I'll ever let her take you again. And neither will Natalie, right?" His eyes begged Natalie to agree without the need for answers.

He breathed a sigh of relief when she said firmly, "Belle, look at me, sweetie. *No one* is going to take you away from your daddy. Or me. I will do whatever it takes, *whatever* it takes, to keep you safe. Okay?"

Belle's eyes searched her face, then his, before nodding and nestling her head back on Natalie's breasts. She slipped her thumb into her mouth and sank into a deep sleep between one breath and the next, escaping terrible memories the only way she knew how.

When Natalie's questioning eyes met his again, he whispered, "Let's get her snuggled in the living room and I'll tell you the story while she naps. The pizza should be ready soon and we'll wake her in a bit to eat and decorate."

"Of course."

He was seeing a glimpse of the mother-bear she must have been with her son. Such fierceness had filled her eyes when she'd told Belle she would do *anything* to keep her safe, and that protective aura still hovered around both of them. He imagined she'd done absolutely everything possible to save her child, devastated when her best wasn't good enough.

She cradled Belle in loving arms—and they were loving, at that moment—her face a Madonna mixture of pain and ecstasy. The pain no doubt of remembered loss and the ecstasy of holding a sweet-smelling little girl's chubbiness against her heart.

Zach leaned over and slid his arms under her thighs and back. "Hold tight."

She squeaked and tightened her hold on Belle when he lifted her into his arms. "You can't carry both of us!" she whispered.

"Sweetheart, you can't possibly weigh a buck ten, and Belle is just a little munchkin. I packed more on my back overseas in a hundred twenty degrees. I think I can manage lil ol' you and the kiddo."

Her eyes snapped to his, and he stopped. Stood stock still as their gazes met and he felt the lock on his heart snick open even more. That mixture of affection in her eyes for his child seemed to bleed over for him.

Her gaze warmed and something beyond her usual blend of desire and irritation broadcast to him. Something his own eyes and heart seemed to recognize and reciprocate.

He'd never believed in love at first, or even second or third sight. But was that what he was seeing in Nat's eyes? Maybe not full-on, full-fledged, but it sure looked like more than just affection. They'd been spending several days a week together—for several weeks, heck, almost three months—while he ferried her back and forth to PT. Shared meals, and occasionally helped her move something around in the house that was too heavy for her, lent a closeness and intimacy that had been growing as time passed.

God, he hoped she was catching up to what he felt for her. His tumultuous feelings must have shone in his gaze, her eyes widening before she glanced away.

❅ ❅ ❅

THE STORM of emotions rolling through Zach's eyes mesmerized Nat. If she didn't know better, she'd swear there'd been a glimpse of love. Nope, had to be imagining things. They'd been spending time together each week, and she'd suspected his feelings for her were growing, but she had no interest in love.

Loving someone resulted in a shattered heart when things went sideways. Nope, she refused to love anyone ever again. Well, except for Calum. Her cousin was really her brother of the heart, and she loved him to pieces.

Unfortunately, she'd discovered just in the past twelve hours she *did* have an interest in Zach—had felt the affection that had been growing the past few months come roaring to the front. He was handsome and sexy as sin. Compassionate. A fabulous, devoted father. A good, faithful friend to her cousin Calum. A good friend to her, if she'd only let him.

The kind of man who fell into the *too good to be true* category.

No way would she act on her attraction or desire, though. She wanted nothing to do with loving a man again, even if that man made her burn for him. Besides, she wasn't the least bit ready to open her heart to his daughter. To any child, for that matter. Anyone who loved Zach would need to love Belle, too. And really, that's the way it should be. She wouldn't respect him—feel *any* affection for him—if he wasn't a devoted, loving father who put his daughter first.

She held Belle tight as he set them on the plush recliner. When he lifted the little girl from her arms, she fought the urge to take her back and never let go. This was not good, *so* not good, becoming attached to either of them.

They both had the ability to break her heart into little, tiny pieces. If that happened, she'd never find all those pieces. Would *never* be able to put her heart back together again.

She watched enviously as Zach snuggled Belle on the couch and tucked Mr. King under her arm, then draped a raggedy Winnie the Pooh blanket up and around her shoulders. She tensed when he pulled a footstool over and sat facing her.

He glanced back at Belle, then turned and leaned his forearms on muscular thighs, gray eyes boring into hers. She couldn't pull her gaze away from the sexy ridges of his thick quads, clearly defined under the soft denim.

When she tore her eyes away and met his again, it was to see a flash of humor and a crooked grin. He'd caught her checking him out and was pleased, if the smug look on his face was anything to go by.

Her face heated as she prodded him for the story. "Why was Belle so upset?"

The grin faded, and the heat in his gray eyes turned stone cold. "Belle's mother and I never married. We dated for a couple months, became intimate. She seemed perfectly normal. No red flags. The relationship wasn't going anywhere though, and I didn't want to lead her on. I'd thought I could fall in love with her, only to realize it was just a desire to *be* in love. To start a family."

He glanced again at his sleeping daughter before continuing. "The day I'd planned to break if off with her, she told me she was pregnant. We'd been careful. No way should she have gotten pregnant. Apparently, she'd realized things weren't heating up the way she wanted them to and, I discovered later, had put pinholes in my condoms. She got her wish and was furious when she realized I wouldn't marry her just because she was pregnant. I told her I would be a part of the child's life, and would pay child support—heck, even shared custody—but she wanted all or nothing. She apparently wanted a free ride; didn't want to work, and wanted me to support her."

Nat shook her head. "I'll never understand why a woman would want to trap a man. You can't build a relationship on lies and manipulation."

"Exactly. She tried for the next six months to get me to change my mind. When she realized I was having none of it, she said if I didn't give her ten grand, she'd disappear and I'd never see my child. Showed her true fucking colors."

Zach stood and paced, fists clenched, and broad shoulders bunched. "In her last few months of pregnancy, her behavior became increasingly erratic. I wasn't even sure she'd make it full term. She'd taken to partying with a rough crowd, hanging around people doing drugs. I was never sure if she was indulging, but thankfully, Belle showed no symptoms of fetal alcohol syndrome or drug withdrawal after she was born. Her mother was with men she let slap her around and rode with them when they were drunk. It terrified me she'd get herself and the baby killed before she gave birth." He scrubbed a hand over his stubbled jaw and sat again.

Nat took his hand and squeezed gently, and she realized it was the second time she'd touched him voluntarily. The heated, affectionate look in his pale gray eyes was a stark reminder she needed to keep her distance. Emotionally and physically. But not now. Not when he needed solace from dark memories.

❅ ❅ ❅

SPARKS OF lust mixed with his growing affection for her when she brushed her thumb across the sensitive back of his hand. He turned his palm over and laced their fingers together, squeezing back to show his appreciation.

"Fast forward to the day after she gave birth. She signed over her rights and walked right out of the hospital. We didn't hear from her or see her for almost three years. I was sure she was out of our lives completely."

He hated remembering that dark time, but she needed to understand. She'd be with them for a few more weeks. If Belle had another scare and he wasn't home, Natalie should know the history, so she'd know how to handle it.

"Belle was watching TV on the couch and I'd run upstairs to grab Mr. King for her when the doorbell rang. She knew better than to answer, but we'd been expecting Calum. She ran to the door and unlocked it just as I looked out the upper window and saw someone on the porch. This was before I installed those deadbolts higher than she can reach." He felt his heart skitter as if reliving the terror he'd felt.

"I didn't recognize her mother at first. She was skinny as a rail, her face pockmarked. I found out later she'd been tweaking; was hooked on meth. I looked down just in time to see her grab Belle and make a run for a van idling at the curb. I busted out the screen and went out the window, down the roof, then down the porch railing and hit the street running as they were driving away."

When Natalie flinched, he realized he'd been squeezing the heck out of her hand. That's all she needed, for her hand to be hurt, along with her already injured leg. He pulled her palm to his mouth and pressed a soft kiss in the middle in apology.

"I found out later she and her tweaker boyfriend, out of the blue, had decided it was a good idea to grab Belle and sell her to fund their addiction. To sell *my baby!* Called the cops and Calum showed up before they arrived. Your cousin knows some guys, a security team made up of buddies from our MARSOC days, and he called them for help. I'd at least gotten the license number and model of the van. We took off on our own and found them four hours later, using info from Calum's buddies, in a shack on the eastside ready to cinch the deal."

"Hey," Natalie said softly, bringing him back from dark memories. "Hey, she's right here. Safe. Take a breath, Zach. Finish the telling, then we'll decorate the tree. Don't go down that *what if* road. Believe me, it does nothing but suck you in and spit you out in pieces."

He did as she said, knowing she was talking from painful experience, and took a deep breath, then blew it out slowly. Her calm, sea-green eyes snared his gaze, and he jolted to realize it was the first time her eyes weren't turbulent or unbearably sad. Somehow, in listening to his telling of what could have ended tragically, and her comforting him, Natalie may have recovered a piece of her soul.

"Cal entered the back while I knocked on the front door. Her boyfriend answered with a gun and I took him out right there. Cal cold-cocked her and put her down. The bastard with the money tried to make it past me. He won't be walking again. I've kept in touch with the prosecutor's office, and unfortunately she's up for parole next year. I hope they keep her, cause if she ever shows up here again making trouble, she'll go down."

Nat uncurled her fingers from his and stroked a finger down his jaw. "So, the doorbell sometimes triggers memories of that day?"

He sighed and nodded. "Usually only when she's tired. I was going to disconnect it, but the doctors said that wouldn't help her deal with it. Or heal. They reminded me that when Belle is visiting someone else's house, those doorbells will more than likely work just fine. Better she learn to deal with it at home."

"She's so fortunate to have you for her daddy, and will move on from this, you know. As young as she was, she'll forget more and more of it as she gets older. Besides, she has your love to hold on to."

"I'd do anything for her." He scrubbed a hand down his face, realizing it was the first time he'd ever really shared how he'd felt, or all of the gritty details of that day. Sure, Calum knew because he'd helped save his little girl, and his sister enough of the details she'd be extra careful, and as protective as Zach needed her to be when Belle stayed with her. It was so cathartic to bare his soul, to let Natalie see how it ate at him—that he hadn't been able to protect his little girl.

Maybe it would even help her understand that sometimes bad shit just happens. That it wasn't her fault her maniac of an ex had kidnapped them. Or that she'd lived, when her son had not.

Zach brushed curls from her face and cupped her cheek in his hand. "I've never shared everything that went down that day with anyone, or how it's affected me. Thank you for understanding and comforting her."

He became aware of her soft hand in his, of the silky skin of her cheek against his palm, and suddenly molten awareness swarmed through his veins. Of her as a woman. He found himself wanting nothing more than to drop to his knees and take her in his arms. To meld their lips and feel her soft, bare skin against his.

That path, he knew, would meet with disaster. She wasn't ready for affection, much less getting naked and making love. And it would be making love on his part—not just having sex. Oh, he knew it wasn't full-blown, but he'd been on a long, slow slide the past few weeks, and he just needed to round third base before he slid into home. He needed to control his burgeoning feelings for this woman, so as not to scare her away. To keep it light until her heart caught up with his. If only she'd open herself to love again with him. He'd cherish her—heart, body, and soul.

Soon, he hoped.

Chapter Thirteen

NAT WOKE AGAIN to a throbbing head and aching shin. She felt pummeled as she lay there. Oh, not physically pummeled. Even though every ache and pain pulsed right through her. No, she felt emotionally pummeled.

She replayed in her head Zach's story from the night before. Her heart ached for him, and for Belle. For herself. What Zach and Belle had gone through could have ended just as terribly as Matty's fate.

Last night, Belle had woken soon after he'd finished telling his story. Nat had lost her desire to go hide in her room and had instead stayed in the living room with father and daughter. They'd eaten pizza, and she'd watched as they'd dressed the tree in all its finery and laid train tracks, the vintage Christmas train chugging around the colorful tree skirt.

Much to her surprise, she'd actually enjoyed being part of their family tradition, although she'd wished with all her heart her son had been there decorating with Belle. Had wished they were a family. Handsome husband, son and daughter, loving wife and mother. She needed to get that picture out of her head. As in *now*.

She paused, shock rolling through as she wondered at the absence of the horrific, heartrending pain that normally swamped her at any thought of her son. There was still pain. It would never fully disappear, and she didn't want it to—didn't want to forget her little boy—but it was oddly muted, in the background. Not searing her soul and sucking the very life out of her.

She wasn't sure she was ready to let it go. To rejoin the living. To possibly care for someone else, either sexy alpha guy or cute munchkin. Those two were worming right into her heart, but she just couldn't, *wouldn't,* let them in all the way.

Opening herself to the risk of losing anyone she loved again? Not a chance. It had been horrific to find the man she'd married was actually an abusive monster. She'd divorced his ass and moved on, making a new life with Matty. Unfortunately, they'd released the bastard from prison without letting her know, and he'd found them—had decided they were still his. She'd barely survived the loss of her son. How could she open her heart and take another chance at love? A small voice in her head insisted, *how could you not?*

"I can't love them," she whispered to herself. "Losing them would surely kill me."

"Oh, sweetie, I think you're already on the way to loving that wonderful man and sweet little one. I know I do. Take the chance, Nat. Open your heart again."

Natalie jolted, totally convinced her grandma was haunting her, trying to get her to live again—to pull her from her depression. It seemed Beacon Bay was living up to its magical reputation.

"Grandma?" She waited, her breath hitching as she wondered if she was just imagining things. That she missed her grandma so damned much she was hearing things—but no, Zach heard her too.

"I miss you so much, grandma, and even if I'm imagining you, it still feels wonderful."

A soft touch on her forehead, much like when her gram used to kiss her good morning, had her closing her eyes against the tears welling.

"It's me, sweetie. I'm hanging around for a while, before I go for good. Let your heart awaken to love, Natalie."

"Oh, gram! I'm sorry I wasn't here for you. I'm sorry I stayed away, that I let my sorrow keep me from you."

"Just never you mind talk like that, young lady. I understood—I understand—and love you more than you'll ever know. Now, do as I said."

A knock at the bedroom door jolted her from her musings. She tugged the blanket over her lap. "Come in." She steeled herself, expecting to see Zach and his little shadow walk through the door.

Zach entered alone, looking too sexy for his own good. Ebony curls draped his broad forehead. Equally dark lashes framed his almost silver eyes, the contrast against his tawny skin striking. The man was too handsome, too caring, for her own good. Heck, he was just too darned everything a woman could want. And a threat to her ability to stay detached.

She glanced behind him. "Where's your little shadow?"

"She's with my sister today, Christmas shopping and helping decorate her tree."

Nat didn't care at all for the jolt of alarm that speared through her to learn Belle wasn't in the house. *Was his sister careful enough?* She was feeling territorial about the little girl. Overly protective. *Where was her deadened heart when she needed it? Why was it resurrecting, now?* She attempted to tamp down the concern and fear, but as hard as she tried, she couldn't keep from asking, "How long will she be gone?"

"My sister lives just a few blocks away and tries to take Belle at least twice a month, and for at least one sleepover a month." He grinned. "Gives her a woman's touch and perspective to balance being with Calum and me the rest of the time." Zach gave her a look that said he understood her concern and appreciated it.

Was she that transparent in her feelings? She could tell by the look on his face he knew she worried about Belle. And why wouldn't she be? After listening to his story last night, she just didn't trust anyone else to be as watchful as they were. "She won't let her play out front by herself, will she? She holds her hand when they're out?"

Nat realized she was sticking her nose smack dab where it didn't belong. "Never mind. It's none of my business. I'm sure your sister is careful, or you wouldn't let her take Belle."

❄ ❄ ❄

ZACH COULD tell it upset Natalie that Belle wasn't home. He hadn't expected this reaction. Oh, he knew she was forming a reluctant bond with his daughter—it had been obvious last night. She was softening toward her, and had actually instigated affection.

While decorating the tree last night, she'd pulled Belle onto her lap as he'd topped it with his mother's porcelain angel. A tradition in his family dating back ninety years. Same angel, every generation. When Belle was an adult with her own family, it would adorn her tree.

He'd watched from the corner of his eye as Natalie had rocked Belle and smoothed a maternal hand down her hair. Watched her drop her cheek to the top of his little girl's head and close her eyes on a sigh.

A mixture of affection and old pain had filled those glass-green eyes when she'd opened them and met his gaze. She'd offered a small smile, then scooted Belle off her lap and handed her a Santa ornament to hang—the moment gone, but not lost.

He walked to the bed and sat on the edge, his leg cocked so his knee brushed her thigh through the covers. He expected her to pull away, heartened when she did nothing more than fiddle with the edge of the quilt.

"Randa is very careful with Belle, sweetheart. She's like a mama bear when they're together."

"Does she have kids of her own, then?"

"Nope, no kids. She's single. Director of a women's shelter. She's around confused and abused kids—and women—almost every day. I trust her with Belle's welfare, emotional and physical."

Natalie's sigh of relief wasn't lost on him. He understood completely her concern. The year after Belle's abduction, he hadn't let his daughter out of his sight. He wasn't sure what he was going to do when it came time for school. Maybe home school and arrange for supervised play dates for socialization.

He quelled her nervous plucking at the colorful quilt by laying a hand across hers. When she did nothing more than still, he laced their fingers together. Her eyes snapped to his, her clear green gaze filled with what seemed to be desire and fondness. He was sure she didn't know her eyes broadcasted her every thought and emotion. If she did, there was no way she would ever look at him.

After their time together last night, acting like a family around the tree, he knew he was on the home-run slide to loving her. He'd been depriving not only himself, but Belle, from a woman's love all these years, just because he'd been afraid to trust again. Afraid to trust his heart. And if he was completely honest with himself, he realized recently he'd been holding a torch for this woman since he'd spent that week with her at Cal's bedside in the hospital.

He'd fallen under Natalie's spell back then, and even more so since reconnecting. His daughter was also falling under her spell, missed a woman's hugs and attention—especially since Grandma Edna had passed. Oh, she got attention, received plenty of hugs and attention from his sister, but that seemed different to him. It was only a couple of times a week, and she was firmly in the aunty role.

Natalie didn't know it, but she was in for the campaign of a lifetime. He'd spent the night unable to sleep, unable to think of anything or anyone else. Her warmth and caring. Her sensuality. Her sense of family, as evidenced by her relationship with her grandma and Calum. Her devastation over the loss of her son.

The way she'd opened up to Belle last night to reassure his little one seemed to overcome her previous desire for distance, and she was now exhibiting mama bear tendencies. He knew in his soul if there'd been any way at all for her to have saved her little boy, she would have done it.

That she harbored such guilt was unconscionable and something he needed to help her let go of, while he convinced her to love him as he was coming to love her. Not love at first sight, but counting the week years ago and the past months, his love for her was growing by leaps and bounds.

Keeping her gaze captive, he leaned in and brushed his lips over hers. Her eyes drifted closed before she jolted and snapped them open again. Her luscious mouth formed a perfect O before she jerked her hand away and whispered, "What was that for? What are you doing?"

"I'm exploring, Natalie. This thing between us. I know it's only been a few months since we reconnected, but I've never been as sure of anything in my entire life."

"Wha…? What are you talking about? Sure of what?"

She was practically shouting at him and all but quivering in agitation. He'd hoped for a different reaction, but this was prickly Natalie he was dealing with. He had to hope she'd come around.

He'd seen the affection, the longing looks she'd sent his way when she thought he wasn't paying attention, and those actions convinced him she wanted him as much as he wanted her. Emotionally *and* physically.

He wasn't one of those skeevy guys who couldn't take no for an answer, or who pursued a woman when she clearly wanted nothing to do with him. But he was the type of man to recognize self-destructive behavior, and also to recognize when someone was interested, even if they didn't want to admit it. If he truly felt she wanted nothing to do with him, he would keep an emotional distance—as fricking hard as that would be—and care for her until her house was back in order and she could walk again.

But that wasn't the case. She not only wanted him, he was sure she *needed* him—and Belle. Now he just had to wear her down and convince her to give them a chance. Easier to do with her living in his house, that's for sure.

He leaned in for another quick kiss, then jumped up and reached under the blankets to scoop her into his arms. "Let's get you to the bathroom. You must be desperate about now."

He stilled when he realized he had a handful of warm, soft bare thighs across his forearm, dressed as she was in nothing but a thin tank top and boy-short panties. After a quick glance down, it took all his strength to bring his eyes back to hers. "Um, I thought you'd have pj's on. I'll help you into the bathroom. Get ready for a drive, okay?"

He ignored the initial daggers and confusion in her eyes, zeroed in on the heat that started swirling in that vibrant green, and deposited her next to the sink with one slim hand holding the edge.

As hard as he tried to keep his eyes on hers, he just couldn't stop his gaze from dipping down to take in her beaded nipples. Or the long expanse of smooth thighs and calves, ending at remarkably sexy feet tipped with hot-pink toenails.

He swallowed hard and swiped a shaky hand across his face as he backed out of the bathroom, hoping she missed the sight of his cock pressed right up against his zipper in its attempt to get to that lush flesh hidden under those revealing, skimpy boy shorts.

A low, feminine voice whispered in his ear after the door closed.

"Don't let her dodge you, Zachary. She loves you and that sweet little girl—she just doesn't recognize it yet."

Zach didn't know if he'd ever get used to a ghost talking to him, but he gave a decisive nod and whispered back, "I'm on it, Grandma Edna."

❄❄❄

NAT DREW a shaky breath, trying to ignore the butterflies in her stomach. *What the heck just happened?* They'd been talking, and he'd swooped right in with those sensuous lips of his. Brushed them in tantalizing strokes across her own.

And just about graced her with what would have been her first orgasm in over five years. With nothing more than a kiss! Shew, but that kiss packed a punch. She took a deep breath and admitted the truth—he'd been giving her heated looks for several weeks. Had been affectionate, concerned and caring. *Was he actually pursuing her?* Part of her wanted nothing more. The other part, the part that had been in hiding for years, wanted to run far, far away.

She really needed to get back to her own house—to ignore the ghostly words of her gram—but the fire marshal wasn't even close to finishing his investigation, and then the fire damage would need to be dealt with before the house was livable again. They apparently had a backlog of investigations, and would get to it when they could. Maybe she could stay in a hotel, even if she couldn't walk yet. Where she could just bury her heart again and not worry about being—falling, she corrected—in love.

Not that she loved Zach. Or Belle. But, oh God, she was falling under their spell. *Could love be far behind?*

She awkwardly used the bathroom and washed up as best she could. She wasn't up to trying for a shower and just made do with a warm, wet washcloth. What she should do, she thought, was tell Zach she wasn't going.

Being alone with him in his truck, driving wherever he had in mind, was too intimate. And too darned tempting without Belle as a buffer.

She had every intention of doing just that, too. Until she opened the door and his hopeful, affection-filled eyes met hers. What seemed right just moments ago now seemed more akin to kicking a puppy.

Although no one in their right minds would accuse Zach of being puppy-like. Nope. More like a sexy shapeshifter from a romance novel. One with storm-gray eyes that could entice you and devour your resistance with just one look.

Her resolve melted like sugar in a hot pot. "Fine, let me get dressed and we can go." It wasn't the most gracious acceptance, but she was suddenly *drowning* in feelings, with no life preserver. A shiver tap-danced on each vertebra up and down her spine. For the first time in what felt like forever, she was going to do something because it made her feel good.

Chapter Fourteen

ZACH PULLED AWAY from the house with Natalie settled in the passenger seat, unable to believe she'd agreed to the drive. It had been a spur-of-the-moment idea born of wanting to get her away and do something for no other reason than it was fun. To whisk her away somewhere she couldn't hide away from him, wouldn't dwell on all the losses she'd endured over the past few years.

Besides, it was also self-preservation. If they'd stayed in the house without Belle, he'd have been far too tempted to revisit what the delectable Natalie looked like sans clothes.

He glanced over and a shaft of heat speared through his core to see her eyes practically eating him up before snapping up to his, realizing he'd caught her checking him out. "What's going through that gorgeous head of yours?" Her eyes widened at the compliment. He figured she'd just have to get used to them.

She shook her head before saying, "Nothing I'm willing to share right now. Where are we going? How much longer?"

"You sound like Belle. Are we there yet?" The pain that lanced through her eyes made him wish he could bite back his words. He'd bet the bank her son used to ask her that. He reached across the seat and laced his fingers with hers. "I'm sorry, sweetheart."

It surprised him when she squeezed his hand back and held on instead of pulling away. "No, don't be sorry." She sighed and shook her head. "Don't censor what you say."

Her breasts rose and fell on a deep breath. "Matty's gone, and it's time I started remembering all the good times." She raised shimmering eyes to his and the affection glowing in her gaze washed over him like sweet, warm honey. "Instead of only remembering how he was—taken from me. You've helped me remember to do that. Thank you."

He swallowed past the sudden lump in his throat. "You're more than welcome, sweetheart. Don't be mad at Calum, but he told me what happened. To you and Matty. Will you share some of the good times with me? Please? Did he used to badger you when you drove somewhere?" He hoped this didn't backfire on him, but he truly thought sharing her wonderful memories would help her heal, or at least not hurt so much.

She waited so long before responding, he was sure he'd stepped in it by suggesting she talk about her son. He glanced at her to apologize again, and let out a breath he didn't realize he'd been holding when she turned to him with a wistful smile.

"He was only two and a half when he started talking up a storm. We'd get in the car, him strapped in the back, and not even make it a block before he'd ask that question—"*We there yet, Mama*?"

She sniffed back tears, but the small smile gracing her face told him sweet memories were tromping the bad. "We'd play a game. He had to count ten blue cars before he could ask again. Boy, if it was a long trip, I'd try my best to distract him so he'd have to start counting over again. As young as he was, he knew I was tricking him, and he'd crack up about that, too."

"Sounds just like Belle, only I ask her to wait until she's seen five houses with red doors. People don't paint their doors red very often, so there's usually a long time between questions. Although sometimes she just can't wait and one will pop out."

He turned to grin at her. "Back to your question about where we're going. I thought we'd drive around the pockets of town famous for their fancy Christmas decorations, then end it with a picnic in the truck, in the park at the end of town. They have a huge pine, fully decorated."

He pulled her hand up for a kiss and kept hold of it as he lowered their still clasped hands to the seat between them. She shot him a wary look, but didn't pull away. *Progress*, he thought. However small, it was progress.

Zach pulled into a cul-de-sac to see a Santa and his reindeer atop a two-story roof, right next to a skinny red-brick chimney. He was happy to see a grin wreathe her face.

He nodded at the steep roof. "Don't you wonder how the heck they got that up there?"

She grinned at him and replied smartly, "I'm wondering how the big guy gets down that little chimney."

He cracked up and grinned back. This was the Natalie he'd known was under the grief and pain. He'd thought her beautiful before, but it mesmerized him how stunning she was when her eyes lit up and those full, sweet lips widened into a genuine smile, revealing her peekaboo dimples. They made the circuit of homes and businesses, coming upon another over-the-top display.

"Can you believe that one?" Her giggle was infectious. "I can't even guess at the number of lights. I bet it tempts the neighbors to cut power to the house just so they can get to sleep at night."

He laughed right along with her. "I can't even imagine how they get everything put up! It must take forever. You can't tell where one decoration ends and the other begins. What's up there next to Santa? Is it holding a carrot?" He loved when she about dissolved into laughter.

She leaned forward to peer out the truck windshield and gasped, then turned to pin him with a mock stern look. "That's an elf, not a bunny! I have no clue what he's holding. Oh my God, the ears on that poor elf, and he's holding a candy cane, but it's orange! I bet Santa brings this guy coal in his stocking for that one."

Zach chuckled as he turned the corner and headed for the park and their picnic. "Hope you've worked up a hunger. We have cold fried chicken, potato salad, and mud cake from Bake It, Girl. They have the best desserts in town, hands-down."

She groaned in pleasure and his pants grew tighter at the crotch as he thought of her groaning just like that when he slid home between her legs. He couldn't stop his own groan, imagining the wet heat that would wrap around every inch when he buried himself deep.

The look she shot him and the pretty blush covering her cheeks told him she'd realized *his* groan wasn't about food at all. If she cared to look lower, she'd see his dick long and heavy in his pants. Something he just couldn't seem to gain control of around her.

❁ ❁ ❁

NAT GRINNED at something Zach said and reveled in the ache in her jaws from laughing so much. It was an eye-opener to realize just how much a shadow of her former self she'd become, as Zach drew her further out of her self-imposed shell. He'd done nothing more than be himself, which she continued to discover was pretty darned irresistible.

Who'd have thought, in just a few months, I'd become addicted to this man's smile? To his innate sense of goodness. His pure love for his daughter. His smoking-hot body and way of looking at her that made it clear he'd like to get naked and busy.

And his touch.

Shew! He'd not only single-handedly pulled her out of her own personal hell of depression, he'd stoked the fire in her libido till it was a raging inferno.

Oh, but it wasn't just that he wanted her. Nope. The affection she caught glimpses of when he looked at her was dangerous to her resolve to stay detached. She refused to interpret the emotion that broke through his gaze every so often. The one that looked suspiciously like love.

Ridiculous! He couldn't possibly love her after spending one-week together years ago, and then the past several months. Surely it took longer than that for someone to fall in love?

She ruthlessly smacked down that small voice in her head, clamoring to be heard. The one that said *liar, you're falling in love, too. Maybe even already there.* She ruthlessly smacked that little voice back and vowed to play it cool, keep him at arm's length, and be back in her house in just a few short weeks, prickly and alone again. *Isn't that what I want, after all?*

Surely she could resist him for that amount of time. Although, what the heck was she thinking? Intimate drives and picnics were *not* the way to stay detached.

She loved—no, *liked*—pretty much everything about the big man. Who wouldn't, for God's sake? He was a sexy, confident, intelligent, protective alpha-guy with a nurturing side. Not to mention a loving father. *Wasn't that what every girl dreamed of?*

It made her wet just thinking of getting horizontal with him. Heck, it made her wet just thinking of holding hands.

"Hey, Nat. Where'd you go? You were thinking pretty hard there for a minute."

She realized he'd been trying to get her attention while she'd been mooning over him and lecturing herself. "Just thinking what a great drive this has been, that's all," she lied smoothly, glancing at him across the bench seat.

"Uh huh, that's why..." His voice trailed off and he glanced knowingly at her pebbled nipples, clearly visible through her lacy bra and silk tank.

Warmth rushed across her face when she realized her fantasies had caused a predictable reaction in her body. Her nipples were hard and tingling, and she knew only Zach could make that ache between her legs go away.

She threw him a disgruntled look. "It's your own fault, big guy." Not wanting to continue down that road, she nodded her head at the back seat of the truck and ordered, “Hand over the picnic basket and feed me.”

She realized she’d bit off more than she could chew when, instead of doing as she asked, he leaned across the long bench seat. Slowly. Giving her plenty of time to tell him to get lost. Apparently, her self-preservation was at an all-time low. All she could do was sit there, deer in the headlights, and wait to see what he’d do.

When his lips met hers, her brain short-circuited. He didn’t dive in like she expected. No, he seduced and coerced with gentle nips, then laved the little sting away with the very tip of his tongue. It was an amazing sensation. One she wanted more of.

He was back to brushing those full lips against hers, working from one corner to the other, then spent an inordinate amount of time on her sensitive upper lip. When his thumb tugged down on her chin, she didn’t even think of resisting.

She granted him access, his tongue sweeping in to mate with hers. In, around, and out to slick across her lips. She tingled from head to toe and all the good parts in between as she pictured his wicked tongue lapping at her girl parts, and had to clench her thighs again when an orgasm threatened.

When his tongue slipped through her lips, she lost it—was nothing but pure sensation. As if he could read her mind, his big hand slipped under her tank, fingertips tantalizing her abdomen before cupping her breast, the thin lace of her bra no barrier at all.

She arched like a cat into his callused palm, wanting, wanting. She wanted him to lay her out on the seat and have his wicked way with her. Lord, how she’d missed being touched. And God! No one had ever touched her like this before. With such sensuous demand. Such honest desire.

Her hand landed on his huge pecs and her fingers danced over every muscled ridge and valley—brushed over his own beaded male nipple. He shuddered, and it amazed her how much this sexy man wanted her.

Her other hand slipped over those bulging biceps and cupped the strong column of his neck to hold him to her. The windows fogged, protecting them from anyone crazy enough to brave the frosty park.

She didn't object when he nipped at her chin, then spread little kisses down her neck before pushing up her silk tank and lacy bra to expose her breasts, trailing kisses down the slope of one to *finally* latch onto a puckered nipple with his lips.

She gasped, then groaned in ecstasy. Had no idea there was a direct link from her nipple straight to her clit. She rocked on the seat as that part of her pulsed at every lap of his wicked tongue and suction of that hot, wet mouth.

With a mind of its own, her hand slipped from his neck, down over his amazing pecs again, and continued its path to map that enticingly ridged abdomen before cupping his hard-as-steel cock. It stunned her to realize he was long enough to almost push out the top of his jeans.

❄ ❄ ❄

ZACH ALMOST shot off at the first brush of her hand down his abdomen. It had been a close thing at the first touch of their lips, much less the combination of his mouth on her lush breast, that pebbled nipple under his tongue—not to mention her busy hands.

Add her nimble fingers wrapped around his cock and it was almost a done deal. His breath whooshed out as he threw back his head and grabbed her wrist, fighting to keep from coming right then and there.

"Wait. Stop. Sweetheart, I'm gonna embarrass myself if you keep that up. I haven't blown in my jeans since I was in my teens. Damn, you get me hotter than molten lava."

He leaned forward till their foreheads touched, planted a soft kiss on her mouth and hoped the park was still as empty as when they'd arrived, but couldn't tell with the truck windows fogged.

They needed to stop, or he was going to lay her out on the seat and sink himself between her legs—or come just from her fondling hands. He knew the minute she started thinking too hard about what they were doing. No way did he want to hear her say she regretted their passion.

He cupped her breast again and brushed the pad of his thumb across the still pebbled tip, loving her response when she arched again into his caress. "I love the way you respond to me. How you're soft…" he gently squeezed the lush mound, then brushed the hard little nub again, "and hard in all the right places."

"Ohhhh, look, ahhhh, Zach…"

"Natalie—sweetheart. Please don't push me away and deny what's growing between us. We enjoy, respect, and want each other. We practically combust when we're within five feet of the other. And when we touch? Damn, woman! Don't give me reasons why this won't work. Why we shouldn't explore this. Let's just enjoy our picnic." Another kiss. "Pick up Belle." Another smacking kiss. "And see where this goes." He looked her in the eyes, not too proud to plead. "Please, Nat?"

He smoothed a hand down her hair and planted a gentle kiss on her cheek, letting her know with his eyes he'd be deaf to any rebuttal—unless she truly didn't want his attentions. Considering she had a hand still wrapped around his dick and her eyes were soft with affection, he knew she was as interested as he was.

He suppressed a grin when she jerked her hand away and huffed at him, belatedly pulling down her bra and tank top to cover those lush breasts and tantalizing pink nipples.

She held his eyes before hers slid away, and confessed in a whisper. "I'm afraid, Zach. How would I survive, opening my heart and losing either or both of you?"

"I know, sweetheart. We can work around that. I'm confident enough for both of us, if you'll just trust me?"

Her small nod of acquiescence felt like he'd won the most priceless prize in the world—hell, in the universe.

He brushed a finger down her cheek and gave a nod of his own. To keep from reaching for her again, knowing backing off to give her time to think was the smart thing to do, he grabbed the picnic basket from the back seat and plopped it between them, definitely needing the barrier to keep him on his side.

"Now, what would you like? A breast?" He shot her a mischievous grin. "Or a leg?" He held out a chicken leg and waggled it at her, winning a small grin back.

Oh yeah, Miss Prickly Pants may not know it yet, but she was going to be his. His and Belle's.

Chapter Fifteen

NATALIE SNUGGLED DEEPER into the covers. It had been two days since she'd lost control with Zach in his truck at the park, and every day since had been a struggle not to give in to the blasted man's routine of seduction.

He was forever touching her. A kiss atop her head in the mornings. A brush of his hand across her hair and down her back. A pat on her butt. A smoldering look across the room. Brushing that studly body against her as he passed, even though there was *plenty* of room to get by.

She knew if she put her foot down and told him she wasn't interested, told him no, he would honor her wishes. But she didn't want to tell him no—and knew she'd been sending him mixed signals.

They'd fallen into a domestic routine, as if they were a little family. He woke her with a kiss every morning, then Belle would crawl into bed with her to snuggle. All soft and baby-sweet smelling. She didn't have the heart to tell her no, either. Had actually started looking forward to their time together.

When it was time for breakfast, he would send Belle downstairs with Mr. King, then help Natalie out of bed and into the bathroom, using every excuse to stroke and touch her. Breakfast would be next, then the quick trip to Calum's for her therapy twice a week.

She'd be sore and grouchy afterward, but he'd kiss, cajole, and entice, turning her into a quivering bundle of lust-filled nerve endings. While she napped, he'd work in his office, and when she arose, she'd work till dinnertime in the makeshift office he'd set up for her in a spare bedroom. She was making remarkable progress on the new book she was editing, as well as shopping for things she needed, since she still couldn't get into her home or to the store.

Belle would read or play quietly for a time, then they would all get together for breaks to play with, or read, to her. It was an enticing routine. One she was becoming much, much too fond of.

As if his emotional and physical seduction wasn't enough, he seduced her with his daughter, asking seemingly innocent question in the evenings. *Do you mind reading to Belle?* Or suggestions to his little girl. *Maybe you could sit on Nat's lap while she reads to you.*

Doesn't he know everyone's heart will break when I move back home?

She sighed at the knock on her door. Right on time, like every morning. "Come in." She tingled to see he was alone and wearing nothing but sweats, riding low on his trim hips, and showcasing his ripped torso. That chest and six-pack oughta be against the law. She'd never survive if he lifted her against those sinful, bare muscular pecs, with biceps bulging.

"Where's Belle?"

"My sister wanted to take her Christmas Eve shopping and picked her up about ten minutes ago. Last-minute gifts for us. Belle's been nagging her for a trip to the mall to buy presents."

Nat shook her head stubbornly. "She shouldn't be buying me presents."

He sent her a reproving look from storm-gray eyes. "She's falling in love with you, Natalie. Of course she wants you to have a present."

She stubbornly resisted that thought, even though she knew in her heart it was true. "She can't love me."

He prowled to her bedside, planted a knee and crawled up the bed till he was straddling her. His eyes darkened to gunmetal and locked on hers. "She's not the only one."

"You can't love me," she whispered. Her eyes burned with unshed tears, and she trembled at the thought of this amazing man loving her. *Her!* "You can't."

It hit her broadside the minute the words left her mouth. She didn't see how Belle could love her. Or how Zach could. Even though she'd fallen head over heels for both of them.

"I can, and do, sweetheart. In the past few months, you've captured not only my daughter's heart, but mine too. I think I started the slide when I met you in Calum's hospital room. I can't resist you, Natalie. Your compassion, strength, beauty, sensuality—your capacity for love even though you don't think you can, or should."

He leaned in and brushed his warm lips against hers, effectively silencing her protests. "Love." Kiss. "You." Slide of his tongue.

Ohhhh, the rat had burrowed his way right into her soul. As much as she'd resisted, she knew in her heart she loved him, too—and little Belle. She just couldn't tell him. Couldn't open herself, or either of them, up to heartache when they realized how damaged she was from losing Matty.

"You don't want to love me, Zach. I'm broken. I can't love you, or Belle, the way you both deserve."

"Don't tell me what I deserve. I know what I want and who I love, and that's you, sweetheart. I'm a patient, stubborn man, and can wait if need be till we put your heart back together."

Unfair! she thought helplessly. "Well, you aren't always going to get what you wa..."

❄❄❄

ZACH CUT her off the only way he knew how. By pressing his lips and his body to hers. It was the first full court press they'd indulged in, and his blood immediately rushed south.

His cock ached—hard enough to cut concrete. This woman just did it for him. No other before her, and he knew from the fullness in his heart and lust in his soul, no other after would affect him this potently.

He knew she had reservations, but also knew from the look in her eyes she was always trying to bank—from her actions—she loved him back. And Belle. He just needed to convince her to trust her heart, even as battered as it was. His eyes held hers and he bared his soul—let every emotion he was feeling bleed through—

and she *finally* rewarded him with a small nod, then a tug as she pulled him back down and took his mouth in a searing kiss.

Ready to come in his sweats from nothing more than her lips and body pressed to his, he clasped her wrists and pulled both her arms above her head, then skimmed his hands back down and whisked her tank top up and off. His breath caught when his eyes landed on the full, perfect globes just begging for his mouth.

He'd caught a glimpse the day she'd hurt herself, and then again in his truck at the park, but man oh man, to be able to look his fill. To see the dark pink nipples bead in excitement took his breath away and turned the ache between his legs to a relentless throb.

"Nat, my god, you're more beautiful than I ever imagined. And I've been imagining—every damn day and long night."

She clutched his biceps, her short nails sensuous pinpricks against his skin. He loved the blush spreading across her breasts, up her slim neck and shading her high, elegant cheekbones. "I have to taste," he murmured huskily.

"Oh, *yes*, Zach."

Unable to resist even a second more, he dipped his head and swirled his tongue over a nipple, just begging to be sampled. A tiny berry atop a lush mound. She groaned as she gripped his shoulders to pull him closer, then arched her back and rolled her hips against his groin.

He jolted at the feel of her grinding against his cock. He could spend hours on her breasts alone, he thought dazedly. No woman had ever captivated him like Natalie did. Her skin was like warm honey, her shoulders and arms lightly muscled. Her waist dipped enticingly, then flared to surprisingly rounded hips, considering her previous weight loss. He'd never wanted, never *craved* a woman as he did this one.

He danced his fingertips down her stomach to the sweet nest between her thighs and cupped that luscious mound as he swallowed her moan. Oh man, he wanted to hear more of that. He slipped his fingers under her panties and brushed his forefinger across her swollen clit, then dipped into her tight, drenched core as he moved his mouth to her other breast.

She rewarded him with another long moan as she rocked against him, one hand grasping the back of his head to hold him against that lush fullness. His mouth busy lipping and nibbling, he dipped a second finger in and curled up against the spot that was sure to drive her wild.

His thumb rubbed circles on her clit, his fingers worked in and out of her tight channel, and his mouth feasted on the hard nub of her nipple. She came apart in his arms, his name torn in a hoarse cry from those sexy lips.

His cock jumped, and when fire roared up his spine, it was a fight to keep from shooting off before being buried in her hot center.

"Oh, Zach! Right there. Yesss! Don't. Stop."

She bowed against him, thighs shaking through her orgasm, before she collapsed in a boneless sprawl. His eyes locked with hers and he jolted at the love shining from those gorgeous green-gold eyes before she masked it and snuggled her dewy face into the crook of his neck to nip his shoulder.

His little wildcat wasn't worn out at all. Looked like, *thank you God*, she was just getting started.

He leaned back, then dipped in to savor her sweet lips, their tongues dueling as her hand delved under the waistband of his sweats. At the first brush of her slim fingers against his cock, pre-cum beaded on the swollen head, and it jumped eagerly against her hand.

When she wrapped those playful fingers firmly around his hard length, he thought he'd died and gone to heaven.

"Nat," he rasped, "unless you want this over before I'm buried in you…" His voice trailed off on a groan and he grabbed her hand as it pumped in slow glides from base to head. "God, Natalie, let me suit up, sweetheart."

His cock would have none of being ignored, and Zach became desperate to be buried deep inside her. As much as he wanted to savor every inch of her silky body, he had to have her. Now.

He reared up to his knees, plucked out the condoms he'd stashed in his pocket, and tossed them on the covers. As he pushed his sweats down and off, his cock bobbed back up, begging for action. He swept her boy shorts down those sleekly muscled legs, careful of any lingering pain in her shin.

He was glad he'd had the foresight to shove a couple condoms in his pocket that morning. Foresight or wishful thinking. He grabbed one, tore the wrapper open, and had it rolled on before she could blink. No way was he giving her time to have second thoughts.

He pressed a swift kiss to her full mouth, covered her body with his, lined up and shuddered as he slid in a bare inch. She was so tight he was afraid of hurting her, even if she was drenched in her own juices. He clenched his jaw and stopped. "You okay?"

"No! I need all of you."

He heeded the demand in her tone and slid home a scant inch at a time, holding fast against the urge to erupt from the clench of her hot core against his cock.

"Don't move Nat." He panted, his muscles straining as he tried to control the urge to pound into her until he blew the top off his head. Both heads.

One hand wrapped around the curve of her hip in a tight grip, the other grasped her shoulder to keep her still, but she would have none of that and wrapped her good leg around his ass, pumping her hips till the friction about killed him.

"Zach, I need you to *move*." Any other time he'd grin at her demanding tone, but all he could do was grit his teeth, ruled by his cock and the feel of his balls tight against her firm, round ass.

He pulled out, then pushed back in just as slowly, close to losing it completely as the walls of her core deliciously abraded his cock. This was better, so much better, than he'd imagined.

He jerked when she pushed against his groin again, sending a zing of electricity down his spine and into his cock. "If you don't get moving, I'm going to, to…"

It was right then he realized two things. Nat was as explosively sensual as he could ever ask for, and she was going to make him pay if he didn't get busy.

Leaning down, he nipped her shoulder, then laved the sting away when she jolted. Sliding his forearms under her back and clutching her shoulders tightly, he pumped in a rhythm she apparently loved, if her moans and tossing head were any sign.

Zach gave himself up to the ecstasy of her sheath, holding him in a grip so tight and hot, he didn't know how he'd last more than a minute. Not wanting to find his pleasure before her, he released one shoulder and reached between them, toggling her swollen clit with the knuckle of his forefinger. Her cry of pleasure told him he was on the right track.

She flew right over the edge, burying her face in his neck to mask her voice, hoarse with sensual ecstasy. The rhythmic clenching of her orgasm had him right behind her, shouting out his own release as he grabbed one hip and ground as deep as possible, pulsing until he was sure he had nothing left in reserve.

Still half hard, he slumped against that lush body, careful to keep from crushing her. They were both slick with sweat and her pebbled nipples poking against his chest had his cock pulsing and lengthening for round two.

He pulled out carefully and tossed the condom in the bedside trash, then rolled back and tucked her head into the crook of his shoulder as he wrapped her in his arms. He loved the way she sighed and snuggled against him.

"I love you, Nat. There's no going back for me now."

Chapter Sixteen

NAT COULDN'T BELIEVE Zach would play such dirty pool. Catch her warm and soft from sleep, then blow her mind with such powerful lovemaking.

Then to pull her into his arms and declare his love again, when she didn't have the energy to argue, was just low. Although if she was being truthful with herself, she'd have found the energy to argue—if she truly wanted to.

His prowess in bed amazed her—he'd been even more than she'd ever dreamed of. The man took her from zero full-on past a hundred in no time flat. Whenever she'd read love scenes in the romance books she edited, she always figured the authors were just making things up when they talked about seeing stars and losing control. Now that she'd lived the fantasy herself, she knew better. Boy howdy, did she know better!

She wanted more of that, and soon. Didn't mean she was ready to accept his love or admit she felt the same, though. Didn't know if she'd ever be.

A pat on her butt got her attention. They'd napped for a good hour, drove each other crazy again, then slept the early part of the afternoon away.

"How about a shower? Belle is due home in about an hour, and I promised her pizza and a Christmas movie. She wants to see *The Santa Clause*. You up for it?"

She stretched against him and watched his eyes go molten with desire. Enjoying her newfound ability to drive him crazy seemed wrong, she thought wickedly, but maybe a little punishment was due.

She stretched again and squelched a smile when his eyes caressed her nakedness, then narrowed in speculation. She could tell he didn't know whether she was torturing him on purpose, or not.

"A shower sounds good. You can wash that spot on my back I always have trouble with."

She scooted to the side of the bed and sent him a sultry look while she waited for him to scoop her up, although she was now fully capable of walking short distances on her own again. She felt in equal measure shy and exhilarated to be stark naked with him.

It was next to impossible to keep her eyes from drifting over all that masculine perfection. When he stood next to the bed, she drank him in, from his broad, strong shoulders, to those mountainous pecs, then down to those abs that were drool-worthy washboard showcased between a wickedly defined Adonis belt. Then that enticing trail of hair pointing down to his…

Her eyes widened, and she wondered how the heck he had fit. He was impressive, even flaccid. Although, as she admired that part of his anatomy, it hardened and rose again, like a sword pointing to the heavens. And he'd certainly taken her to heaven, she thought with a shiver.

"Keep that up, sweetheart, and you won't make it off this bed. We have just enough time for a shower before the kiddo gets home. Do you really still want to be naked and sweaty?"

Her eyes shot to his, sudden embarrassment washing over her. She'd never been a hedonist, but wow, she wanted nothing more than to stay in bed with him for, say, the next year. Or two. Then maybe she'd be able to look at him without wanting to jump his bones.

"You can't look like that," she grumbled with a wave of her hand, "and expect not to be stared at."

He grinned and scooped her into his arms, the bulge of his biceps causing another shiver to run through her. She'd always been a sucker for muscly men. The more muscle the merrier.

She leaned in and brushed her lips across his, jolting when his cock jumped and brushed her butt. He narrowed his gray eyes at her and devoured her mouth as he strode into the bathroom and carefully set her on the seat in the shower.

Nat knew she was heading for heartbreak, but couldn't make herself regret their intimacy. He'd realize soon enough she wasn't a suitable candidate for a girlfriend, or mother to his daughter. Not as damaged as she was inside—both heart and soul. But they could have these moments in time.

She watched as he adjusted the water, unable to keep her hands to herself. He'd unleashed the sensual woman in her that had been hiding for *years*, and now that she'd escaped her bounds and let the little hussy out to play, play she would. Her fingers wrapped around that steel shaft before he could blink, pumping until he shuddered and groaned, grabbing her hand to stop her.

"Sweetheart, you've no idea how close to the edge I am whenever I'm near you. Add on flashing that glorious body at me and actually touching me? Like a match to fireworks, baby."

He turned, his cheekbones flushed with passion, and reached into the drawer next to the sink, drawing his hand back with a flat packet between his fingers.

"Suit me up, baby, but be fast." He shot her a wicked grin. "On a hair trigger here, even if I did just have you."

His storm-gray eyes flashed with desire as she tore open the packet with her teeth, pulled out the condom, and took him in hand.

She leaned down and pressed a kiss to the swollen mushroom head before slowly rolling the rubber over and down, down that long hard length of pure pleasure. A glance at his clenched jaw and fiery eyes told her he was a hair away from coming, just from the touch of her hands.

He cupped her face in his big palms and laid the sweetest kiss on her lips. With one hand on her elbow, he steadied her as she stood, then palmed her butt and lifted so his cock nudged her slick opening. She let out a squeal and wrapped her legs around his hips, just above his delectable, muscled ass.

Her moan vibrated in her chest when the thick head slid in far enough to hit and sensuously abrade that special spot. His moan echoed hers when he shot home, balls deep. She couldn't for the life of her hold back a cry of pleasure as he pumped in and out, his cock owning her.

He met her keening cry with a shout of pleasure as he pumped once, twice, then buried deep as she felt his orgasm pulse, clenched tight inside her core. It was a darned good thing he was holding her up, or she'd collapse in a puddle at the bottom of the shower.

❄ ❄ ❄

ZACH COULDN'T believe how combustible they were together. He'd never come even close to being this turned on, this on fire, for a woman. Not in all his days.

He pulled out, aftershocks zinging up his spine as her tight core reluctantly released his cock.

"Turn around and sit, honey. I'm about to fall on my ass." He leaned in to brush a kiss across that sensuous mouth and trailed kisses down her neck.

Much more of that and he'd be taking her against the wall again, he thought. He pressed one more kiss to her jaw and forced himself to stand on shaky legs. "Where's that spot on your back you can't reach?"

He leaned back and caught her grin as she no doubt remembered taunting him with washing her back. *Damn, but she was sexy.* How'd he get so lucky, anyway? Knowing time was ticking and Belle would be home soon, he nevertheless dropped to his knees and proceeded to make her happy and delirious with his tongue on her sweet spot.

He was grinning like a pirate thirty minutes later when he'd tucked a dry and sated Natalie back in bed, sound asleep. He'd worn his beautiful mermaid out and she was down for the count.

Not a minute too soon, when his sister's voice from the front hall heralded Belle's arrival. He dropped a kiss on her pretty nose and jogged downstairs to greet his daughter, his heart soaring in the clouds.

Chapter Seventeen

NAT WOKE TO whispering next to her bed. She cracked an eye open to see Belle whispering to Mr. King. "Daddy said not to wake her up, Mr. King, but I just wanted to be sure she was okay. That fire was scary—and why is she asleep? She's going to be so mad when she finds out. I don't think she'll like me after, and now that I love her, I don't want her to hate me."

Nat's heart thumped when Belle said she loved her. She swallowed hard, beating back tears of joy and sorrow, wondering if there was any way they could actually work as a family. The little girl was such a sweetheart to worry about her. She listened as Belle not-very-stealthily crept from the room, and on the heels of that thought felt like the biggest bitch for making the little girl feel she didn't want her around.

She knew she'd been snippy and standoffish in the beginning, enough to convince Belle she didn't like her, when in reality it had been the thought of liking her too much that brought forth those reactions. She was rusty when it came to how to act around kids. But over the past couple of weeks, they'd bonded, reading together and snuggling.

Oh, for God's sake, who on earth am I trying to kid? She could lie to herself till they colonized Mars, but the truth was she not only liked Belle, she loved the little girl. And had slid into home base with Zach, too. She, who'd never believed in love at first sight—or in a scant few months—had fallen for Zach and his daughter. Head over heels.

Belle's words skipped through her head again. *She's going to be so mad when she finds out.* Natalie thought she knew exactly what Belle meant by that. She'd had plenty of time to think about how the fire had started, and had just that morning remembered glancing at the porch while climbing out of the bathroom window, seeing the plug for the Christmas lights securely in the socket. The plug that had been lying on the porch since she'd moved in, the cord like a snake trailing behind it.

She hadn't been the one to plug the lights in, and Belle had been in the backyard. One plus one equaled flames and smoke. She'd bet her newfound love that Belle had plugged in the lights, determined that Nat enjoy the holiday, causing something to spark and kick off the fire.

She felt sure that's what the determination would be when the fire department finished their investigation. But she couldn't be mad at Belle. What kid didn't want bright, sparkly things at Christmastime? She hadn't planned to say anything to Zach or Belle, hadn't wanted to make either of them feel bad or guilty.

But since Belle was aware, Nat had to clear the air with both father and daughter. She also refused to continue to be coddled. She appreciated Zach's care, but knew her own limitations and felt clear-headed and steady enough to at least get out of bed on her own. Not that she hadn't enjoyed the heck out of being wrapped in his arms, held against those beefcake pecs and huge biceps.

Nat slid her legs over the side and climbed from bed, her leg giving barely a twinge and her head pain-free. She snagged her borrowed yoga pants from the chair and slipped them on, padding quietly into the hall and down to Belle's playroom.

She wondered briefly where Zach was until she heard the distant clacking of a keyboard from his office a few doors down. As she paused in the doorway of Belle's playroom, her heart was heavy to hear the little girl still worrying with Mr. King over whether Nat would be mad to find out she'd caused the fire.

"Hey," she said softly as she walked through the door. "Is Mr. King excited about Santa coming tomorrow?" Belle looked at Nat with wide eyes, as if a growling mutt ready to bite her head off had just prowled through the door.

"He thinks maybe Santa won't come 'cause Mr. King and I have been bad."

Nat felt the lock on her heart snick all the way open with affection and love at the look of abject misery on Belle's little face. She couldn't stand to see the little girl eaten up with guilt over something innocently done, simply because she loved Christmas.

She sat on the loveseat next to Belle and brushed a hand gently over her hair. She knew the best way to handle this was not to draw it out.

"Sweetie, I'm not mad at all about the fire. I know you think it's your fault for plugging in the cord, but it's really not."

It shocked her when Belle burst into tears and jumped into her arms. “I'm sorry Nat-alie. I dint mean to, honest!”

“Shh, it's okay Belle. Shh, don't cry sweetie. I'm fine, I'll get the house fixed and best of all I get to spend Christmas with you and your daddy.”

It heartened her when Belle's tears lessened to sniffles and her sweet little face turned up to stare through glistening eyes filled with love.

“You pwomise you're not mad?”

Nat closed her eyes and tucked Belle's head under her chin, rocking her as she reassured, “Not even a little bit, sweetie.”

When Nat opened her eyes and blew curls out of her face, she saw Zach in the doorway, a wide smile on his handsome face, and the affection shining from his gorgeous eyes letting her know he'd heard it all, and was grateful for how she'd handled Belle. She smiled back.

“How are my ladies doing today?”

Belle snuggled against Nat's shoulder and gave a watery giggle. “I'm not a lady, Daddy. I'm just a little girl!”

Zach strode to the loveseat and braced on one knee, leaning over to give Belle and then Nat smacking kisses, and whispered in her ear, “Thank you, sweetheart.”

As he smoothed a broad palm down first Nat's curls, then his daughter's ebony hair, he said, “My sister's locked herself out of her house. Do you think you and Belle will be okay while I run over there to let her in?”

Nat looked down at Belle. “I'm sure we'll be okay while you're gone.” She glanced at Zach, her heart beating faster to see the glint in his eyes.

She glanced back at Belle and asked, "How about I read to you and then we watch a movie when your daddy gets back?"

Belle's eyes lit up, and she jumped off Natalie's lap, tugging on her hand. "Yes!"

"I'll get you settled downstairs before I go." He leaned closer, and she closed her eyes on a sigh when he pressed his lips softly to hers in a lingering kiss full of promises for the future.

He scooped Nat up in those powerful arms and said, "Come on, pumpkin. Downstairs with you both. And no shaking Christmas presents, either of you!"

He got them snuggled on the couch, and Nat blew him a kiss as he left the house, hugging Belle to her breast as she read one of the little girl's *Lowly Worm* books. They both enjoyed the worm's antics and were looking forward to watching *The Santa Clause* when Zach returned.

He'd thought of everything, even setting a pot of hot chocolate and cookies on the coffee table, admonishing her to be careful when on her feet, and with a last kiss had dashed out the door.

She read the last line of the book and pressed a kiss to Belle's honeysuckle-scented hair. "Are you ready for hot chocolate and cookies, sweetie? Then I'll start the movie and we can snuggle on the couch again. Your dad won't mind missing the very first part."

"Yes! I love when his little boy and the elves break Santa out of jail! That's the bestest part!"

Nat chuckled at her enthusiasm, looking forward to seeing the movie again. There'd been no Christmas movies watched in her house since she'd lost Matty, and it amazed her to feel the warmth of fond memories drowning out the usual pain when she thought of her little boy.

She poured chocolate into the snowman mugs and placed the cookie plate on her lap. Belle snuggled against her side again and nibbled on a cookie. Nat told reindeer jokes to pass the time and Belle giggled, then looked up and said, "I love you, Nat-alie."

Tears burned her eyes as she enveloped Belle in her arms and whispered back, "I love you too, sweetpea." She wiped tears from her cheeks as Belle went back to munching her cookie. It's just that simple, she thought. *Why can't I love Belle and her daddy? What law says I have to be miserable the rest of my life? Why am I fighting this, anyway?*

What a time to have a life-changing epiphany, she thought with a huff. *And why not?* It *was* the season of miracles, after all. She brushed a hand down Belle's tangled hair and turned back to set her cocoa cup down when shattering glass in the kitchen made them both jump.

An urgent voice came from the couch next to them. "*Nat, Belle, quick. Run!*"

"Gram Edna!" Belle whispered. "What was that noise, Nat-alie?"

Momentarily distracted by the fact it didn't surprise Belle to hear her gram's voice next to them, she turned and asked, "Can you hear my gram?"

Belle's turned toward her, eyes wide with terror. "Yes, she reads to me at night and keeps me safe."

Natalie had no time to dwell on that revelation, because it sure sounded like someone was breaking into the house through the kitchen door.

She rose to her feet and pulled Belle up with her. "I want you to go lock yourself in the bathroom, Belle. Don't come out for anyone but your daddy or me."

"No, I don't want to leave you!" she wailed.

Natalie cringed, knowing if anyone was in the house, they'd have heard the little girl.

"Sweetie, I don't know what that noise was, but until I find out, please just go into the bathroom. It'll be okay."

A raspy voice from the hallway door contradicted her reassurance. "Well, bitch. I don't know as how things are gonna be okay."

Nat stood and pushed Belle behind her. The woman in the hallway was rail thin, her gaunt face riddled with acne scars. She had a feeling she knew *exactly* who they were facing.

Belle tugged on her tank top and whispered, "That's the bad lady. Don't let her take me again!"

The woman pinned her eyes on Belle. "Bad lady, my ass. I deserve a present at Christmas, and you're it this year, brat."

Rage filled her. *No one is taking this little girl!* If she had to die protecting her, she would.

"Zach is going to be home any second," she bluffed and fervently hoped she was right. That he didn't get caught up visiting with his sister. "You need to get out before he returns. You don't want on his bad side, believe me."

"Who you kidding, bitch? I left him a little present. He's gonna have to fix that flat tire at his dear sister's house first."

"Didn't you learn your lesson the last time you tried this?" Nat wasn't the least bit interested in her answers, but figured keeping her talking was her best bet for now.

"I been watching for a few days, waitin' for him to leave you two alone. Knew he'd eventually have to leave the little brat with gimpy you, and BAM! I'd have my chance." She crooked a finger at Belle and rasped, "Get over here, brat. We're leaving."

"Not going to happen." Nat never wished more for a baseball bat or a tire iron. She glanced quickly around the room and didn't see a thing she could use.

Best bet was to get Belle out of the house and hope a neighbor was home, or Zach would miraculously appear.

Nat turned and pushed Belle ahead of her toward the front door, exaggerating her limp and glad the woman evidently didn't realize her leg was much better.

She'd apparently seen Zach carrying her around and thought Nat's injury was worse than it actually was. As she scooted Belle out the door, she turned at the sound of the woman following them.

The only good thing was that the crazy bitch thought Natalie wasn't a threat and wasn't moving fast to stop her. She leaned down and whispered, "Run next door to Mrs. Maguire's and go right into her house. Go now! Be fast!"

She gave Belle a nudge and watched anxiously as she ran down the porch steps. "Dammit!"

The woman shoulder-checked her, causing Natalie to lurch forward and grab the porch railing to keep from falling. A kick to the thigh of her injured leg almost took her to the ground, and when the woman's fist connected with a glancing punch to her temple, Nat's leg buckled. Seeing stars, she shook her head to clear it. There was *no way* she was losing Belle to this bitch. Natalie made a grab for her as she scooted past and caught nothing but air.

"You don't touch her!" Her scream rent the air, and she prayed a neighbor was outside and would come to their aid.

Belle didn't make it ten yards before the woman grabbed her from behind and jerked off her feet. Natalie roared again in anger and ignored the twinge of pain in her shin and knee as she ran after them, snatching up a garden gnome on her way. "Let her *go*!"

"Nat-alie! Nat-alie!" Belle was pounding her little fists on the woman's shoulder and screaming like a banshee.

Natalie caught them halfway across the yard and smacked the woman upside her head with the sharp ceramic lantern clutched in the gnome's gnarled fist.

As she wrapped her other arm around Belle and pulled, she brought the gnome down on the woman's head again in a crushing blow. Belle came free into her arms and the horrid woman toppled.

Nat clutched the sobbing child tightly to her chest and ran toward the neighbor's house. The old woman never locked her door, and she knew if she could just get inside and lock it behind them, they'd be safe while waiting for the cops.

She'd almost made it to Mrs. McGuire's porch when she heard the squeal of tires and what sounded like a lion's roar. When she glanced back, relief made her dizzy to see Zach jump from his truck and run toward them, veering off to where his ex lay crumpled on the ground.

She grunted as her calf muscle spasmed, and she twisted in midair as her leg collapsed so she would be on the bottom when they crashed and not crush Belle. "Crap!"

She squinted through her pain and saw Zach reach the woman as she was trying to crawl away. He grabbed her arm and flipped her onto her stomach, pulling her other arm behind her back.

He pinned Nat and Belle with stormy eyes brimming with rage and fear. “Are you okay?” he asked hoarsely. “Tell me you’re okay.”

Nat smoothed a hand down Belle’s back, trying to quiet her sobs. She nodded to reassure Zach and whispered, “Shh, it’s okay, sweetpea. She’ll go away forever now. Shhh, didn’t I tell you I’d *never* let anyone take you away from your daddy? Or me.”

Belle turned her sweet, tear-stained face to Nat and wrapped both chubby arms around her neck in a stranglehold. “Don’t ever let me go, Nat-alie. Please don’t ever leave me.”

Natalie fully lost her heart at that moment. It belonged to this little girl and her daddy, and thank God she’d come to her senses and embraced her feelings.

“I’m not leaving you, Belle. Ever.”

She kept Belle snuggled in her arms and watched while a police cruiser slid to the curb and an officer jumped from the car to relieve Zach, cuffing the cussing woman and moving to the side for EMTs to check her out. Natalie hoped she had a concussion, and they put her away for good this time.

❅ ❅ ❅

ZACH RAN over to Nat and Belle, sure he’d lost twenty years of his life when he’d turned the corner to see Natalie smack Jo Ann. To see her defend his child, risk herself like that, filled his heart with fierce pride. She’d fought as if Belle were her own child. He dropped to his knees and wrapped them in his arms.

"Daddy, you're squishing me," Belle complained.

He loosened his hold and leaned back to press a kiss to Belle's forehead, then brushed Nat's lips with his and groaned. "I could have lost you both."

"We're fine, Zach. I promise. Belle's a champ. Aren't you, sweetie? You were so brave."

Zach nodded. "You both were. Let's get you in the house. The police can come in and talk to you there."

Nat nodded and said, "There's glass on the kitchen floor. We heard glass break..."

Belle interrupted excitedly. "And Gram Edna warned us, too!"

When Nat nodded, Zach looked incredulously from one to the other, not realizing until just this second that their sneaky adopted grandma had been talking to and watching over all three of them, not just him and Natalie.

"Your grandma is a hell of a woman, Nat. Apparently she's been haunting all three of us."

At Nat's grin, he grinned back and shook his head in wonder.

"Jo Ann came in from the kitchen," Nat continued. "Must have broken the panes to get in the door."

"I'll put a solid core door in tomorrow—no glass. I couldn't believe it when I saw you running, sweetheart. Thank you for keeping Belle safe." He swept a hand down her curvy waist and tucked her against his side.

"I would *never* let anything happen to her, Zach."

"You were fierce as hell." He shook his head in wonder.

Nat turned burning eyes toward him. "There was no way I was letting her get away with your little girl." Her gaze gentled as she turned shimmering eyes to his daughter. "She's burrowed her way right into my heart."

He kissed her again and hoped *he'd* burrowed his way into her heart, too. There was a question he was dying to ask, but ruthlessly squelched it, brushing a finger across her shin instead. "How much pain are you in?"

"It's pretty sore, but I don't think I actually re-injured anything. Think you can do your he-man thing and carry us both again?"

It surprised Zach she could joke at a time like this. She continued to amaze him with her resiliency. "Sweetheart, I'm just the he-man to do it."

He scooped her into his arms, pausing when she placed a slender hand on his cheek and kissed him softly. He didn't know what to make of the expression in her eyes. Was afraid to hope what he saw shining through was love.

He strode past the pitiful woman on the lawn and up the steps to their home. And it was going to be theirs, dammit, if he could convince Natalie to open her hear to love—to his and Belle's love.

Epilogue

BY THE TIME the police finished with them it was late evening, and Belle was understandably cranky and upset. Zach knew just the thing to help her forget, even if just for a little while.

"Hey, sweetpea." He picked Belle up, and sat with her on his lap next to Nat on the couch. The tree was awash in color, the vintage glass and porcelain ornaments reflecting the colorful twinkling lights.

"It's Christmas Eve. What does that mean?" He glanced at Nat and grinned at her confusion, then back at Belle.

Belle's eyes lit up, and she actually squealed, tiredness forgotten in a blink. "Pwesents! We get to open one pwesent each!"

She turned to Nat and shook her chubby finger as if scolding her. "Only one. The rest are for tomorrow."

Zach laughed outright to see Nat's answering smile. He rose and nestled Belle next to her, then found the two presents he and Belle had bought for her, along with his present to his little girl.

"Not so fast, Santa's helper," Nat instructed. "Grab those two in the back with the reindeer prancing on them."

He cocked a brow at her, wondering when she'd had the time to shop. Although, come to think of it, he remembered her getting a few deliveries the day before. He'd thought they were just things she'd needed personally, or for her work.

"That's better," she said with a grin when he had them in hand and was sitting next to them.

He glanced at the tags and saw his and Belle's names in bold print. He distributed the presents and followed orders when she motioned for them to unwrap their gifts.

Belle clapped her hands and giggled when a Mrs. King stuffed lioness, minus the fluff of a mane, along with a cub, came tumbling from the box. "Oh, Nat-alie! Thank you, thank you! Now Mr. King has a Mrs. King and a baby. Now they're a family! Just like us!"

Zach grinned at his daughter's enthusiasm and the tender look on Nat's face at Belle's proclamation. He tore into his present, and his breath caught to see a small, framed print of a man, woman, and child building sandcastles on the beach.

"It's us, isn't it?" he murmured as he leaned in for a kiss, his eyes never leaving hers as his heart tripped with hope when she nodded.

"Beautiful. I love it. Thank you, sweetheart."

❄ ❄ ❄

NAT REVELED in the look of love shining from his eyes. When he said beautiful, she realized he was talking about her, not his gift. She blushed under his scrutiny and kissed him with all the newfound love filling her heart.

"Nat-alie's turn, daddy." Belle turned sweet eyes to her. "Open my pwesent next."

"Okay, sweetie." Nat tugged the snowman wrapping from her gift, wondering what it was. When she lifted the pretty tea mug and read the inscription, her eyes overflowed and she choked back a sob.

"I adore it," Nat said on watery sigh. She looked at the sweet little face of the precious child next to her and held out her arms. "I love you, Belle. Come here, sweetie."

When the little girl climbed into her lap, she wrapped her up tight. Nat's eyes met Zach's, and she gave a wobbly smile, then looked at the mug still clutched in her hand. The words blurred but meant the world to her. *The most perfect mommy ever,* it read.

Zach lifted Belle onto his lap, handing Nat his gift to her. "Now it's my turn."

She set about opening the small, rectangular box. After lifting the lid, it took her a moment to realize what it was.

An old-fashioned silver charm bracelet lay snug against black velvet. Dangling from the delicate links were five charms. She fingered the ornate M, trailing her fingers across the other four before turning to Zach with curious eyes.

"M for Matty, sweetheart." He stroked a finger down her cheek and leaned in for a kiss. "Z for Zach, B for Belle."

His heart in his eyes, he murmured, "The Victorian house is *our* house, and the heart is because you own mine."

Nat looked down to see Belle grinning like a loon at them, then leaned over to brush her lips over his before giving the little sweetie a smacking kiss on the top of her head.

"I'm glad to hear that, Zach, since you own mine, too."

His eyes darkened with love and passion at her words.

Nat pulled his head down and laid the sweetest kiss on him. "I love you Zach. You and Belle are my everything."

"I love you so much, Natalie. We both want you, need you, to stay here with us."

Natalie took their hands in hers and held tight. "I'd love nothing more. You and this little munchkin of yours made my heart whole again. I'm right where I belong."

At the sound of muffled giggling, a soft feminine laugh, and masculine chuckle, they look towards the Christmas tree to see three ghostly images.

Nat gasped, happiness, relief and sadness swirling through her heart and mind. Her grandma and grandpa were bookending her little Matty, who released the gnarled hand of his loving great-grandma to wave and grin at her. "*Love you mama. Grammy and Grampy are babysitting me!*"

She was aware of Zach and Belle exclaiming next to her, knowing they could see the ghostly tableau themselves.

Her gram gave a soft, loving smile and reassured her. "*We're taking good care of him until we're all together again—a long, long time from now. We all want you three to be together and happy. Bye babygirl. We love you."*

The three winked out, like stars in a new sky, and Nat realized instead of her heart breaking, she finally had a modicum of peace, knowing her little guy was happy and in loving arms, until he could be in hers again.

Her glance at Belle, then at Zach revealed worried eyes, and she rushed to reassure them.

"I'm okay. Seeing Gram and Gramps are watching over Matty fills me with so much relief. I'll always miss him, and wish he was here in our family, but I love you both so much—and can't wait for us to start our lives together—as a family."

Loving lips met hers, and a chubby hand patted her cheek clumsily.

"Love you, Nat-alie," a little voice exclaimed.

"Love you so much, Natalie. Forever and ever," Zach vowed.

Her mind settled. Her heart filled to overflowing. She smiled softly and said, "Love you both more than I can say. Forever and ever."

The End

Thank you for reading Loving Her Holiday Hero, Book 1 in the Beacon Bay Magic series! I hope you enjoyed Nat and Zach's slide into love as they become a family with little Belle.

Are you read to join Randa and Kasa on their spine tingling adventure in Book 2 of the Beacon Bay Magic series? Grab your copy today from one of the major print or e-book vendors.

Dear Readers

I hope you enjoyed Loving Her Holiday Hero! If you think others would also enjoy Zach and Nat's (and little Belle's) story, will you please consider recommending it to a friend, and/or leaving a review? Just a couple of sentences will do on one of the popular review sites, either where you purchased the book, or perhaps Goodreads or BookBub.

Who knows, your review just might be the one to encourage them to one-click and give it a try! I can't tell you how much I'd appreciate it.

Many thanks for reading my books! I absolutely love crafting characters—both good and bad—to share their hair-raising and ever-so-steamy encounters with you.

Slàinte Mhaith and happy reading!

Much affection,

Fiola

Connect with Fiola

Visit my Linktree landing page to sign up for my VIP mailing list, connect on social media or and visit my website. I can't wait to 'see' you there!

https://linktr.ee/fiola_faelan_author

https://fiolafaelan.com

About Fiola

FIOLA HAS ALWAYS loved to read and write, with her first mini-story crafted at age five. She's come a long way from chubby fingers wrapped around crayons putting words, albeit misspelled, to paper.

Nowadays, Fiola loves to dream of romance, and has exchanged crayons for a laptop so she can bring *Shift into Romance* to life. She lets her characters go crazy so they can indulge in paranormal sexy-times between the pages, where alpha men embrace their wild side and strong, independent women learn that muscles, magic, and fangs not only help them survive, but also find sensuous satisfaction while doing so.

She grew up a devout tomboy, tackling every tree on the block when Silicon Valley wasn't even a gleam in San Jose's eyes, hitting life full-tilt barrel-racing her Appaloosa as a teen, running parkour across the Morro Bay breakwater, surf-fishing in Hawaii in her twenties, and walking barefoot on the beach dreaming of romance.

Nowadays, she's always on the lookout for ideas for her next story; that next place to bury the body, or lock lips with an uber-alpha, muscular man who knows his way around a woman's body and embraces feminine strength and all that entails.

She kicks-ass, takes names and crafts characters in the beautiful Portland Metro area of Oregon, where she cohabitates with her amazingly talented son and equally talented daughter-in-law, and their most affectionate cat Nudge.

A Word from the Author

From the National Coalition Against Domestic Violence statistics, on any given day, there are 20,000 plus phone calls placed to domestic violence hotlines nationwide.

When there is a gun in a domestic violence situation, the risk of homicide increases by 500%.

This subject is important to me because I was married to a violent man for a short period of time, and when the verbal abuse became physical, he was out the door the same day.

However, not all women are able to extricate themselves as readily as I did—for a variety of reasons. In this story, the heroine has lost her child because a violent ex reappeared and kidnapped them. This is not an anomaly, and happens far too often.

If you feel so inclined, you can make a donation to this organization: https://ncadv.org/donate

Trademark & Copyright Acknowledgements

THE AUTHOR acknowledges the following trademarks of products mentioned in the book:

Bino & Fino
Winnie the Pooh
Dora the Explorer
Lowly Worm
YouTube
TikTok
The Santa Clause
The Snowy Day
Velcro
Zootopia